Second Time ... Shame on Me.

A Novel by
Erica Martin

Second Time Shame On Me
A SherrifMatt9 Book/Published by arrangement with
The author

Printing History
First Printing/January 2003

ISBN: 0-9727498-0-2

Dedication

It would take me a lifetime to thank each and everyone that has helped me fulfill my lifetime dream of becoming a published author. But first let me start with Mrs. Virginia Burnett, my grandma. You have always been the one pushing me, dragging me, threatening me to use my God-given talent and for that I am ever so grateful. I dedicate this book to you. Thank you for your unbiased opinions and criticisms of "Second Time...." and the encouragement you gave me when I had writers block. I love you.

To my husband Demetrius, thank you for being my inspiration, without you there is no me. To my sons Gary, Demetrius (Mookie) and my step-daughter Trevion, thank you for understanding when my writing time cut into your playtime, Mama loves you. To my Mom and Dad and my sisters Kim, Phyllis and Monique (yeah you too!) I couldn't have done this without you all and I appreciate all the advice. No matter how many times I bumped my head, you guys were still there when the smoke cleared. To my girls, Shannan, Lanika, Tina and Donnie, you are the stars that guide me when I am lost. To all my aunts and uncles, Grandma Sallie and friends (too numerous to name), thanks for having my back. To Kyle and Monica, I know you are smiling down on me, I feel it.

To Matt, where do I begin? I could have never done this without you and I cannot even begin to thank you enough. You have been a friend, a mentor, and a counselor and so much more to me through this process and I appreciate you so much. Your guidance and encouragement have made this all possible and I will forever be indebted to you. Con mi corazon y alma, muchas gracias mi amigo.

To anyone I left out, know that you are not forgotten in my heart.

Love,
Erica Martin

Foreword

I grew up in Detroit. In some ways it was different than any of the other big cities, in other ways it was the same. It was different because of its history of change and how it handled the migration of many Southern Blacks who came north to Detroit to better their family's lives. Many came looking for jobs in the Automotive Plants, and the large Industrial Factories. They were deluded in the south to come north for free jobs. They were used as " Strike Breakers and Scabs" for unscrupulous businessmen. It was the same as the other Big Cities because of the many –Pot-holes of Delusion- and –Missed Opportunities- experienced by African Americans in all of the "Big Cities".

Many of the young women grew up with the hope of attaining a better life than the one that they saw their mothers live. I think the Northern attitude was affected by the need to feel "rich" "To be important". Not to be associated with the Southern poverty and discrimination that they had run from before. Clothing and cars became symbols of stature and people were willing to do almost anything to attain it. The women knew that the man with the most ends could meet their needs and if her man had a big car and a fat pocket (Star Qualities), then she could reap the benefits too. Being a "Baller's Woman" was almost as good as being the "Baller" yourself. The men began to understand the power of the "almighty dollar". And, that they could have whomever they wanted and just about anything else that they wanted, by having what everybody wanted.

This is the story of four young women who grew up in Detroit. These young women come from different backgrounds, but in the end they faced the same struggles as their mothers. They experienced the same feelings of frustration, anger, and hopelessness. There were the same

5

men who took out their societal frustrations out on their Black Women.

The Four Women in this story sought to find the answers to breaking the cycle of confusion. And, to overcoming their individual shortcomings they each pointed out about one other.

The book shows the kinship, devotion, and loyalty that these women shared. Despite the individual differences the love that they had for each other provided the source for their growth and security.

It is my hope that this book will define and illustrate the message that. "We all will make mistakes, but we don't have to continuously make the same mistake over and over. If we allow another person the opportunity to abuse us when they have already demonstrated that they will. Then it is not the fault of the abuser, but our own.

Erica Martin

Author

Prologue

Sydni Jamison was a pretty girl raised in a middle-class family with two younger sisters. As a kid, the other children could never pronounce her name, so everybody just called her Sid. She was now grown with a child and on her own trying to make it. She worked a day job, and at nights at a Bar. She depended heavily on her tips to make ends meet. She was also attending college at night.

Mya McPherson like Sydni was attractive and smart. She was very observant seldom missing anything that passed before her. She was also trendy. Mya had a kid, and often had problems with her baby's daddy who had no problem going up side her head.

Blake Morris was a young lady married to a man 18 years older than herself, who also had a serious drug problem. She didn't receive a lot of attention at home, and with her weight problem she was lost in a sea of self- pity. Blake believed that the key to changing her outlook and her life was in losing weight to a size that she felt would attract her husband Jay, and be pleasing to her friends.

Ariel Adams like Sydni worked a day job, and at the Bar at night. She had a respectable job as a Bank Clerk at Standard bank. Ariel had issues too. She had a shaky relationship with a cheating man. Ariel was always critical of her girls being used by men, but was unable to control her own weakness for her cheating man. These four women who were so different in outlooks, were all in one accord whenever any of them were threatened.

Erica Martin

8

CHAPTER 1

"If I had my way the world would be perfect. There would be no cheating husbands, no----no-good baby daddy's, and no violent athletes". Sydni commented as she looked away almost as if she was talking to herself.

"You mean no men!" Melanie who was wiping down the bar asked.

"Nah!! I ain't ready to go that far. Can't live with them and I damn sure can't live without them! I swear I can go all night....like a trucker. That's probably why I'm where I am now." Sydni turned facing Melanie as she profoundly clarified what she meant.

"Girl, if he calls me one more time, I am going to scream". Sydni stated as she took her turn at wiping down the other end of the bar.

Melanie who worked along side of Sydni just shook her head. She had heard it all before. Sydni had just left the man that every other woman would dream of.

Sydni was a pretty woman in her early twenties. She was built on a slender frame, but very shapely. Her light brown olive complexion was a mixture of her father who was a Bi-racial mixture of Black and Puerto Rican. And those of her mother who was a mixture of Black, Indian, and White with Indian like features and straight hair. Sydni wore her hair which was dark brown, at shoulder length. From a distance her hair looked black. She could change her entire looks by the way that she wore her hair. Sydni weighed in at a comfortable 138 pounds which blended well with her 5'5" frame. She was slim but had all the curves where they were needed. She was the oldest of three children.

Sydni wasn't married but she did have a baby boy, his name was Eric, after his dad. He was two years old and very active. Their relationship didn't survive so Sydni was raising little Eric with big Eric's help. She moved on with her life and started dating Syrus a professional Basketball Player who played in another city. After a few months, Sydni didn't feel like that was working out for her so she ended that relationship. Her girlfriends couldn't understand why Sydni would cut a catch like that loose. But that was theirs to wonder and Sydni's to know.

Sydni often worked two jobs to make ends meet. Right now though she was working at a Bar called, "On The Mile" a local bar that had a reputation for attracting a fairly decent clientele. It wasn't unusual to see local businessmen, high rollers in the Pharmaceutical (Drug) business, and from time to time Professional Athletes. So, it wasn't unusual to see a bevy of beautiful women. Sydni had her own name for them she called a lot of them "Hoochies". These were women who were specifically out to land a big fish by getting all in their face as exhibitionist.

Sydni met Mike at the bar. She really hadn't paid too much attention to him during the night. He wasn't one of those brothers that would knock you off your feet the moment that you saw him. From the standpoint of looks, he was just an average brother.

Sydni was all business when she was tending bar. She had made a name for herself as one of the fastest barmaids in town. On this night she was really earning her money.

Mike had been watching Sydni all night. He and his crew had already consumed $300.00 in liquor and he had just ordered another bottle of Moet champagne. This was one of many that he had ordered during the night. Of course he was

Sydni's number one customer at that point, as long as they could take them down, she could set them up. He had made a few passes at Sydni during the night, but she was too busy with the heavy crowd to concern herself with his flirtation. She really hadn't had an opportunity to kick it with him. She hardly had a moment to break for personal needs. When she saw her first opportunity she took it.

"Melanie, I'm gonna go to the bathroom since the hooligans are all nursing their shots of Hennessy and Coronas".

"Hurry up girl! I gotta go too"! Melanie told Sydni as she hopped from one foot to the other.

Just as Sydni rounded the corner to the restroom, she bumped into a gentleman almost knocking the drink out of his hands as he was coming out of the restroom. She was surprised when she saw who it was. It just happened to be the big spending brother with the $300.00 tab who had been giving her the eye all night. Mike was a chunky Mocha Chocolate brother with curly hair. He had his Crew with him and they had been talking shit and drinking all night long.

"Well, you finally got a minute I see". He said as he stepped closer. "My name is Mike and yours is Sydni...I overheard someone trying to get your attention". Mike was all grins and happy at finally cornering Sydni.

"I know, it can get really hectic back there". Sydni responded as she stepped back slightly when she noticed that he was invading her (personal space).

"I'm sorry, is something wrong? Your man must be here". Mike replied with a quizzical look on his face.

11

"No....that's not it at all. I don't have a man perse. I have friends". She said looking him squarely in the face.

"Well, I want to be your friend, if that's alright with you". Mike stated, as he looked her up and down. Sydni could feel his eyes as they measured her up.

In her sexiest voice, she said. "We'll see". She then walked down the hall to the ladies room. He didn't know that she watched him watching her in a Budweiser mirror hanging on the wall. "Yea! I thought so". She thought with a small note of satisfaction. Sydni had no problem attracting men. It was just the kind of men that she attracted.

The long night had finally ended. After giving Sydni a hundred and fifty dollar tip and a napkin with his phone number on it he left with his friends. She promised to call him the next day for a breakfast date.

The other waitresses, all of whom were her best friends, were tripping! They all wanted to know who her new benefactor was. Blake a self proclaimed hypochondriac was being her usual sickly self. After a bout of harsh coughing (highly exaggerated of course) she asked:

"Girl who was the hottie buying the Moet?....Baby had it going on". Blake waited for an answer from Sydni.

Before Sydni could say anything Mya broke in. "I like when guys dress neat like that with the Girbaud hookup and the brown Gucci loafers and the brown leather to match". We could always count on Mya to know exactly what a brother had on and where he got it.

Ariel took her turn at bat. "I know he was looking good, even though he was a little chunky! Sydni, you know he might crush your skinny ass! They all laughed at Ariel's crack on Sydni who still hadn't commented on their questions.

From the back of the bar they heard Melanie's bark. "Alright let's get out of here, some of us want to go home."

The next morning Sydni woke up with a foot literally in her face. It was her two- year old son Eric's foot. He had climbed in the bed with her during the night. She was so tired that she never noticed. Little Eric was her heart. With gentle care she picked him up from the bed and gave him a kiss on his cheek.

"Okay Baby, let's get moving, we have a lot to do today". Little Eric appeared oblivious to it all. As she rushed down the stairs she almost knocked her father over. As a last resort Sydni had recently moved in with her dad to try to save some money. Her parents had divorced a few months before and they didn't want to sell the house. Her mom had already moved out and her dad was about to move, so she volunteered to take over the mortgage.

It took Sydni exactly one hour to get the both of them ready. She knew that it was going to be a good day everything was going to smooth. That was, until she walked outside and noticed that someone had broken into her car and stolen her airbags.

"What the hell? I cannot believe this shit"! She yelled as she paced back and forth in the street. This wasn't the most unusual thing that could happen in Detroit. Airbags were an expensive item in a car. Thieves would steal them by specific order. Little Eric started crying because she was yelling. He really didn't understand what was going on. He could clearly see that him mom was upset. Sydni went back into her house to recuperate and decide her next course of action.

"Damn, everyone is at work". She verbalized out loud. She then remembered that she was supposed to meet Mike for breakfast. She thought for a moment and decided that she had better call and cancel her date. Sydni dug into her oversized Coach bag trying to find his number. As she searched she thought. "This is crazy, I don't even like heavy brothers, and he definitely was on the chubby side". But she decided to call anyway.

"Hello Mike......this is Sydni, remember me?

"Of course I do, how could I not remember a fine specimen such as you? So what's up"? He asked.

"Well, I'm afraid that I am going to have to take a rain check on our date. When I walked out this morning to get into my car, it had been broken into and my airbags stolen".

"Is that all"? Mike asked Sydni.

"Yes, and that's a lot because I have a $500 dollar deductible".

"Then consider your problems over baby. I'll pay your deductible and get you something to roll in until it's fixed. All I'm asking for is breakfast. Do we have a deal"? He asked.

"What? Bet"! She gave Mike her address and he was there in thirty minutes.

True to his word, Mike was there in thirty minutes. He took Little Eric to Day Care first, and then he took Sydni to breakfast. After a beautiful breakfast he took her to the Car Rental place and rented her a sporty little rental. Mike was a fast mover and doing all of the right things in Sydni's emergency situation.

By the time that they got back to Sydni's home, the Tow Truck had already picked up her car. What started off as a catastrophic day had evolved into the discovery of a new friend that she could depend on.

Now back on wheels, Sydni decided to stop by and see her friend Ariel at the Standard Federal Bank where she worked. She was anxious to share her experience, especially the one involving her new friend Mike.

Sydni stood in Ariel's line at the bank until she worked her way to her. "Hey girl... you're not gonna believe what happened to me today".

"No, I probably won't, but tell me anyway". Ariel was always the skeptical one. If there was a negative she would find it. After listening to Sydni's story she replied.

"Usually when something is too good to be true, it is just that". Ariel told Sydni.

"I know, I know! You are always so quick to jump to negative conclusions". Sydni said somewhat disappointed that Ariel wasn't sharing her enthusiasm.

"I didn't say anything negative. I just stated a well known fact and you are holding up my line! She snapped back at her friend with a grin on her face.

"Excuse me......I am a customer and I just made a fat $500 deposit, thanks to my new found friend"! Sydni said with a twist of her head.

"You got problems girl, you need to talk to someone". Ariel laughed as she made her final comment. "Now get out of my line and call me at six. Are you hanging out tonight"?

With certainty written all over her face Sydni replied. "For sure, I'm out"!

CHAPTER 2

Sydni was on a roll. She was attending Wayne State University working on her degree in Marketing. She had a new friend and was driving around in a flashy sport car. The girls had an unwritten rule. Whenever someone new came into their lives, they always provided the 411 on the new man. It served several purposes, one as a bragging point, and the other as a safety measure, in case something happened to any of them.

Mya and Sydni hadn't talked in several days. Sydni needed to give her the low down on her new friend. Since she had several hours to kill before her first class at WSU, she decided to give her friend Mya a call. When she mentioned Mall and shopping that was all it took to get her up and ready to go.

When Sydni pulled up, Mya eyed the new whips with gratitude. "Where did you get this"? Mya asked. After explaining the whole story from beginning to end, she was tripping! She looked at Sydni with a quizzical look. "And he is paying for the rental too"? She asked. "Damm, girl, you gave him some!" Mya commented as a matter of fact.

"Hell no! I don't do one- night stands, plus he would have to do a lot more than rent me a car and give me $500. I got that golden shit! They both bust out laughing.

It was always fun shopping with Mya. She knew exactly what had just come out, and where to find it. Their crew could rock it before everybody else. Sydni and Mya were busy trying on different outfits. Just hanging out and having big fun with each other. Everything was fine until Sydni noticed a bruise on the outside of Mya's arm. She didn't say anything until she saw the inside, which was black and blue.

"What the hell happened to your arm Mya"? Sid asked concerned.

"Oh this! It ain't nothing! Darius and I were playing around last night and he grabbed my arm a little too tight".

"What the hell were y'all playing, Smackdown or WWF"? Sydni asked not really expecting an answer. Mya laughed not offering any further explanation.

"It's not funny Mya, I know y'all weren't fighting were you"?

"No Sid -- quit tripping"! Mya commented as she nervously laughed for Sydni's sake.

"Girl, you know that shit ain't cool!" That was Sydni's final comment on that subject. The girls finished their shopping and information exchange. Whenever they fussed at each other, it was because of their genuine love and concern for their friend's welfare.

"That ain't cute Mya, but it will match that black and blue Mossimo shirt you just bought"! They laughed as they walked out of the store.

It seemed like summer had just started and here we were in the middle of October already! It's funny how things happen so fast. Just as the weather changes, so was the relationship with Sydni and Mike. They had been dating for a whole month already.

As Sydni got out of the shower, she heard the phone ringing. She hurried up the stairs to catch it. It was Blake.

"What's up for tonight girl"? Blake asked.

"Girl, I'm getting ready to go eat with Mike". Sydni answered.

"I guess I should have known that without asking. You two are attached at the hip. Can a friend get a little of your time? Where is Eric"? Asked Blake who was beginning to sound as if she had something on her mind.

"I dropped him off at Big Eric's house......can you believe that?" Sydni's relationship with Big Eric was strained to say the least. The problem mostly was the lack of personal time that he spent with his son. He didn't always come up with support money. She wasn't having any problems raising him it was just that he needed a male role model. Those who knew about the problem insisted that she go down to "Friend of the Court" and apply for support. Sydni didn't follow that advice. She had her own moral values. Her idealistic view was that she shouldn't have to make a grown man take care of his own child. Ideally she was right, but in the real world it didn't make sense unless Big Eric was physically incapacitated and unable to do his part in the support of the child that he helped to bring in this world. She rationalized her views by thinking that what little Eric did for the baby was extra, because she kept Little Eric tight.

Blake was shocked that Big Eric was keeping Little Eric. "I can't believe he's doing that! What's gotten into him"? She asked surprised as hell.

"I don't know girl, I just go with the flow." Sydni responded.

"I feel you, I do the same with Jay". Jay was Blake's husband. He was 18 years older than her and was fighting a lingering drug habit. Blake had told the girls that she didn't find out about his drug problems until after they had gotten married. It had finally gotten to her. She was tired of his lies and of finding his drug paraphernalia. Her major concern was their two children. Blake was under a lot of stress and she reacted to it by eating. Boy did she eat!

Sid realizing that her friend needed her moral support, as well as someone to vent with, she set up a date.

"Well, we will have to kick it tomorrow Blake. I know you are stressed and I'm concerned. But, I have to get ready; I'm running late as usual!"

Just then she heard the doorbell ring. "Oh shit! He is always on time." She was still wrapped up in a towel as she ran to the door.

"Hi, I know, I'm sorry. I'm never ready." Sydni said before she looked up. She was shocked shitless when she looked up and saw who it was. It was Syrus.

"I see....some things just don't change do they? You never were one for timeliness". He said as he pushed his way into her place.

"Excuse me......what the hell do you want? I thought I asked you to stay away from me. I would like for you to leave right now"! Sydni tried to usher him back through the door that he had just stepped through. She tried to shut the door using it as the force to make her point that she didn't want him in there. He wedged his foot against the door holding it open.

"Sydni, you know that I didn't mean to hurt you.....I love you that's all, and I was mad". Syrus explained.

"Sy, we've been over this before. I don't want anything to do with a man that feels he has to put his hands on me. If that is what you do to someone you love, then I'm afraid to imagine what would happen if you hated me. Now leave." Sydni's words were emphatic and clear.

"So why are you rushing me? Are you expecting someone?" Sydni was wise enough to know that she had to handle him with –kid gloves--. That translated into her having to be nice to him if she wanted him to leave. If she succeeded in pissing him off, he would stay just for the hell of it. She knew from experience that he had a fiery temper.

"Well whoever this brotha is.....let him know I ain't through with you, so don't get too comfortable." He slammed the door of his Mercedes 500 and sped off. Sydni was shaking as she closed the door. She wasn't sure if it was from fear of the brisk wind blowing on her naked body, or with what she had just experienced. "What is wrong with these Brothas"? She thought as she went upstairs to get dressed.

The next time that the doorbell rang, she was ready and made sure that she looked out the peephole to see who it was. It was Mike.

"Sorry I'm late baby, I had to make a stop before I got here". If he only knew Sydni thought. He was carrying a
Kids Footlocker bag. When he noticed that she had seen it. He stated.

"Oh, I bought little man something." "Something" turned out to be a Nike jogging suit with matching gym shoes. Sydni noticed that it was the same suit and shoes he had on.

"That's cute Mike, and thank you. Little Eric's over his dad's house right now, but I'll be sure to have him call and personally thank you himself. Let's go".

Mike could tell that something was on her mind, but he didn't want to pry. He wondered if he had gone too far with the shoes and outfit for her son. He had noticed all the Brothers hitting Sydni at the bar and that she hadn't given them any play. He wasn't wasting anytime on this one. Now that he was in, he planned to stay in. Sydni was a cool girl, he thought. She was smart, independent and fine as hell. He had never seen a women wear her hair in so many different styles and look that tight with it. He had already made up his mind that he was hitting it tonight.

Sydni did have a lot on her mind. She was still thinking about Syrus's impromptu visit. He hadn't shown his face in months. What had sparked this sudden display of jealousy? She wondered. She thought about the Pistons and wondered if his team was playing them. Maybe that was why he was in town. Oh well, she thought. "I can't worry about him right now I have two many other things and people on my mind."

Sydni was cruising down the expressway cooling out and feeling good when Mike sprang his plans on her for the night.

"Baby, I thought we could use some rest & relaxation tonight, so I got us a room at the Du'Jour in Ann Arbor. I made appointments for us to get massages".

"You're too sweet". Sydni thought to herself. "Oh well, I can't hold out forever". She surmised.

22

It was obvious to Sydni that Mike had thought this little adventure out well. He had every little detail covered and in place. And based upon how he had been treating her and Little Eric. She didn't feel that she had much of a choice. Besides, maybe it wouldn't be so bad.

Once they were checked in, they hurried to the spa to chill in the whirlpool while they waited for their turn with the masseuse.

"Sid, I know we haven't been kicking it for a long time, but you are my woman right?" Mike was still laying ground work for his project, which was to capture Sydni that night.

Sydni thought for several seconds choosing her words carefully. "Mike, I really like you a lot, but I do have other friends".

"I don't want you to have other friends". Mike snapped back.

"When I say friends, I mean friends. I'm not sleeping with them." She explained.

"So that's what I am then, because you aren't sleeping with me either." He had a good comeback she thought.

"Mike.....can't we just take our time and wait for things to happen?" She asked. That night things did happen.

Every Sunday everyone met at "Mama's" house. It just seemed to be the right place. Sydni's Mama Sharon was probably the coolest mother in the world. (Not smoke weed in front of her cool) just cool in the way that she carried herself, and in the way that she treated her kids and their friends. Everybody called her Mama.

Mama and Sydni had a very unique relationship. She wasn't pushy, nor was she a pushover. Mama knew enough about the world to be able to offer her girls sound judgment on just about anything. Mama was more of a friend than a mother in terms of how comfortable she made Sydni feel. She could tell her mother anything. Which was exactly what she was about to do when her little sister Rimy walked into the kitchen.

"What's up"? Rimy asked as she looked in the refrigerator. "Mama, what are you cooking, whatever it is, it smells good."

"Sausage rice and gravy. Is that alright with you"? Mama asked in a facetious manner. Sydni was minding her own business, but Rimy managed to wrangle her into the act.

"Sid, we have that too much! I know that you are the one that suggested that"! Rimy commented.

"So what, you should try waking up before one o'clock some times." Sydni took a shot at Rimy.

"You think I'm bad, Paige is still asleep". Rimy spoke.

"Mama, you better check on her, she's been sleeping an awful lot lately." That was Sydni's comment to Mama.

"You know she tells you everything Sid. That girl better not be pregnant". Mama said.

Sydni and Paige had a unique relationship. She was Sydni's middle sister and just like Mama always said, she did tell Sydni everything. Their relationship grew even more as they got older. Sydni planned to talk to Paige, but for the moment she was more interested in talking about what had happened the night before.

"I will talk to her Mama, but let me finish telling you what happened last night. Sydni had already started telling Mama about her experience with her new beau Mike. She was anxious to get back to the story. She paused a minute to gather her thoughts again. "So after the massages, we went up to the room. I was all hyped and ready, you know massages do that to you. We get to going and Mama I swear I didn't know he had started! I'm serious Mama". This was in response to the blank look on Mama's face. Sydni had a look of total disgust on her face, which prompted Rimy to bust out laughing.

"Quit playing Sid! I know that you're not telling me –Mr All—is little like that"! Rimy was having more fun out of this than Sydni wanted her too.

"Shut up Rimy! What do you know about little or big things?" Sydni didn't wait for a response from Rimy. "Anyway Mama, I could have died! Why is it that it always has to be something wrong with a brotha? Bad breath or no job or a little dick! Always something." Sydni said shaking her head in disgust.

Mama paused for a moment to allow Sydni to compose herself after her little trip down memory lane from the night before.

"Speaking of jobs, what line of work is this young man in?"

Sydni lied, she wasn't about to tell Mama the truth about Mike's profession.

"I don't know Mama". Sydni got her lie on and it would have gone over pretty smooth except for her little sister Rimy.

"He's a street pharmacist Mama, and he's got it going on." Rimy's mouth was running like a forty- nine cent nylon stocking.

"Shut up Rimy, you don't know what you are talking about"! Sydni shouted to Rimy. Mama just smiled and shook her head she really hadn't paid much attention to what Rimy said in the first place.

Paige finally crawled out of bed and came down stairs where the rest were looking more dead than alive. Before Rimy could say anything she said:

"Shut up Rimy! You know I was sleep!" She screamed out. "You shut up! It's 1 o'clock in the afternoon it's time
to wake up! And besides, you didn't say anything to Sid". Rimy barked out to Paige.

"That's because I only heard your big mouth"! Paige shouted back.

Paige and Rimy didn't get along. There was three years difference in their age with Paige being the oldest, and thought that she should have some control over Rimy. Rimy thought otherwise, she never listened.

Sydni saw this as a good time to corner her sister and have their little talk. "Paige, I want you to roll with me to pick up Eric. I can tell you what happened last night. Pretty soon Sydni would have told her whole family about her experience with Mike. That really wasn't too cool, even she knew that, but it was a thing that they had as a family. There wasn't much that they kept secret from each other, except

26

Paige's present situation. As Sydni was driving along Paige just blurted out:

"I'm pregnant Sid". It was like Paige was so full that she was about to burst the way her revelation came out.

"Oh my god! Why didn't you tell me Paige? You can't have a baby now, you are in your last year of high school." Paige's revelation had left Sydni stunned to the point that she was hyperventilating and was beginning to feel sick. "Okay, stop and think and breathe". Sydni thought to herself. The initial shock was mind blowing. Sydni felt a little guilty at not knowing something was wrong. She was aware that Paige had been avoiding her lately. When Sydni would call the house lately, Paige would make all of their conversations short and to the point, or she would give the phone to Mama. Paige could never keep a secret. It was shocking that she was able to keep her own. Ordinarily if you didn't want something known, you didn't tell it to Paige.

"I'm sorry Sid, that's why I haven't been able to talk to you. I knew that if I talked to you, I would tell you, and I wasn't quite ready".

"So.....are you gonna have it"? Sydni was trying to sort things out and get some direction.

Paige responded. "I don't know what I want to do. Sometimes I think that I do, and other times I don't. I'm scared Sid". Sydni had never seen her sister so scared, and it hurt her to see her in this predicament. "Well, don't worry Sis. Whatever decision you make, I'll have your back. You already know that, so stop worrying. What does Alonzo want you to do"? Sydni asked.

"Sid you know Zo, he is leaving it up to me." "What were y'all laughing at earlier"? Sydni smiled and told her story one more time. They headed home.

The house had filled up and the party was on. Sydni's gang was there. That included Blake, her husband Jay, and their two kids, Mya, Ariel and their kids. Paige and Rimy's best friends Renee and Tasha were there too. It was a typical Sunday at Mama's house.

Things were going pretty smooth until Blake and her husband Jay started their free show. She had looked into her purse for some money and noticed that she was twenty dollars short. There was instant anger, Blake pretty much knew what he had done with the money with him being a drug addict. She was upset because he hadn't asked her for the money, he just took it. " But, on the other hand she thought. If he had asked for money, and I thought that it was for drugs, he would have never gotten it from me"! Sydni listened as her friend vented. "I'm so tired of this shit. I have to hide my money and jewelry because I don't know if he is going to steal it for drugs".

"Well Blake, just think you'll be thirty in a few more years. Do you want to be going through this same shit"? Mya directed her question to Blake, but she didn't try to pin her down. She had been having trouble with her baby's daddy for a while now. Sydni and the girls suspected that they had been fighting again. Mya always had good advice for the others in the group it was usually advice that she herself could use. There was one very unique thing about the girls. They may have shared their problems with each other, but in the end they always made their own decisions.

"I'm moving back to the house on Terry, alone". Said Mya, referring to the house that she owned jointly with her sister.

Blake had enough problems of her own with Jay, but that didn't stop her from offering advice to Mya. "He ain't gonna be tripping is He"? Blake asked referring to Darius Mya's man. "Because Girl, you know how we roll"!

Ariel spoke up. "Look, ain't nobody about to be going up against that crazy ass Darius, girl you better do the right thing and get a restraining order".

"Yeah, and use the same gun he gave you to bust his ass if he comes anywhere near you". Sydni butted in with her resolution.

"Sid you are too ghetto to be as bou-gee as you are"! Ariel commented. "Speaking of bou-gees, guess who called me last night"? Ariel waited for someone to venture a guess. Blake took the bait.

"Ariel the only bou-gee brother you mess with is Antoine". Ariel laughed. "Yep, you hit it on the nose".

"So what's up with –Mr. All That And A Bag Of Chips?- Sydni asked Ariel.

"He's graduating in January and he just got a new job with the state". Ariel answered.

"Oh yeah.....what happened with you two"? Mya asked.

"I didn't tell you"! Ariel asked. She knew that she hadn't told them, and that this was her opportunity to let the girls know what was going on with her and Antoine. "At least two months ago I was over at Antoine's house. I was asleep in his bed when this heffa came over there! This asshole let her in. I found out when I heard her yelling and screaming downstairs, talking about how come he isn't

29

answering his phone or her pages. Then she comes running up the stairs! I didn't have on shit but the sheet, but I was ready to drop the sheet and beat her ass in the buff if I had to. When she saw me, she broke down crying and left. You know I went off on his ass"! Ariel assured them that she had held her own.

"Wait....this no good ass brotha let her in knowing you were upstairs asleep"? Maya asked. "Girl, you should busted out every last window in his house and then his car"! Mya stated to Ariel.

Mya was notorious for window busting! They had rode with her before on a number of occasions on her window-busting missions. She was on a roll now. Once she got wound up she could go.

"So why should you care about him graduating, he didn't give a damn about hurting you or that girl"! Mya protested.

"I know but I still don't wish bad things on him". Ariel answered.

Mya rolled her eyes and stated: "You should".

"Well I don't. Mya you know we have history".

"Ariel, he wasn't thinking about that history when he let that broad come up those stairs with you in the bed. Now was he"?

"Girl, you got a lot of nerve going there, because lord knows you have done the "forgive and forget routine" many times yourself." It was Ariel's time to put Mya in her place.

"Alright ladies, it's not that deep. We don't need to be fighting each other". Blake interceded. At that time Sydni

30

saw an opportunity to diffuse the ill feelings of Mya and Ariel. "Hey, I have to go to Target.

"Anybody else interested"? She knew the mention of shopping would grab everybody's attention.

Second Time ... Shame On Me.

CHAPTER 3

The next few weeks seemed to fly by. Sydni's dad Carlos had not moved out like he had promised he would and the tension was beginning to build between them. His controlling demeanor was starting to make her feel like a teenager again. He didn't permit her to have company over too late, and she had been suddenly designated as the clean-up woman.

Sydni took her dad's domineering treatment for as long as she could stand it. She truly loved her dad, but she had come to the conclusion that she could not live with him. The final straw came when he demanded to know what time she was coming home on Friday night.

"Why are you demanding to know what time I am coming in? Why does it matter Dad"? She asked.

"Well, because I don't think you need to be coming in here at all times of the night. It don't look good, and I think that it is disrespectful"!

"Dad! I am a grown woman…..it really shouldn't matter to you what time I come in. We had an arrangement".

"Well, let me just say this! As long as we are living under the same roof, you will respect my wishes. Is that clear Sydni"? Carlos asked.

"You're right dad. I need my own roof". These were Sydni's last words as she walked out the door.

Sydni couldn't shake the thoughts of her last experience with her dad. She kept seeing him in her mind's eye, and how serious he was. He actually believed that he was right. Then she wondered how Mama had dealt with his strong will. Maybe that's why they're not together she thought. She kept repeating out loud, talking to herself as she drove to the bar. Occasionally she would look to the left or right and see people looking at her strange. They were probably wondering if she was losing or had lost her mind having this great conversation with herself.

"I can't believe this crap, I should have known better in the first place to think that this would work. I haven't saved a dime since I've been here either. I'll figure out something fast because I can't deal with this shit anymore". She ended her conversation with herself as she arrived at the bar.

The bar was fairly quiet, customer-wise that is. DJ KB had his gear fine-tuned and had "Benjamin's " pumping. She liked the lyrics to the song and began to loosen up a little as she listened. "That's what I need some Benjamin's and I'm going to get some tonight"! She sang the song and it made her feel upbeat.

Ariel who worked as additional help sometimes was already there, cutting up lemons and limes. Blake was placing ashtrays on all of the tables.

"What's up ladies? Are we having a party tonight or what"? Ariel was live.

"I don't know, my feet hurt already and it's early". Blake replied.

"Well, if you didn't have on 6 inch heels, that might help the situation". They all laughed at Sydni's crack on Blake.

"Do I look alright?" Blake asked waiting for either of them to reply. Ariel took the bait. "Look don't start that shit Blake, I already told you twice that you look cute."

"I'm almost where I want to be. Give me one week and I promise I am going to get me some 34's". That was the size of the Guess Jeans that Blake was determined to be able to fit in.

"You are fine Blake, really". Sydni's confirmation seemed to have more value to Blake, so she cooled out on that subject.

Sydni placed her purse and coat under the bar as she prepared to get started for the night. She commented: "I need to make some money tonight.....for real! I'm about to move up out of there because my dad is tripping bad".

"Ask Big-Money grip for the money". Ariel suggested. "He just hooked me up for Sweetest day, girl. I didn't show you the two outfits complete with boots and purses, plus a cell phone"?

"Are you serious"? Sydni asked. "Ask Blake". Ariel said. "I swear I don't know what you do to these brothers. I need some lessons"!

The night was flying by. The music was pumping so everyone was dancing. And, of course that made them thirsty, which was good for Sydni. She and Melanie had earned the title of the "Best Barmaids" on "The Mile". They were pretty fast and could usually get to everyone that the waitresses didn't. Everything was going just fine until the fight started. That stopped everything until things settled down.

Sydni was passing one of her customers a drink when Kenny cut the music off. This was the signal that there was some commotion going on somewhere in the bar. Melanie and Sydni struggled to see past the crowd to see what was going on. Tony, the Night Manager was in the middle of the dance floor between two girls, one who happened to be Ariel! Melanie and Sydni ran around the bar just as Blake blindsided the girl who Ariel had been arguing with. The girl had friends too she hadn't come there alone. She had three women with her. About that time, one of the women grabbed Blake from the back by her weave. There was nothing that she could have done to Blake that would have infuriated her more. She took great pride in her weaves.

Sydni and Melanie were already engrossed in their own personal battles with the enemy's friends. Ariel and the woman that the fight started with were rolling around on the floor. It seemed like hours before the bouncers could separate the two teams. The crowd was cheering as the "visiting team" was thrown out, literally. Tony the Manager was mad, but he couldn't help laughing at his "Night Crew". They did have a reputation for sticking together. This wasn't the first time that they had tangled in the bar.

There were no serious injuries to any party. Blake was begging to be excused, so that she could go look at her hair. Sydni had already asked Tony if they were going to keep the bar open after the fight? He said that they would. Ordinarily they would close the bar after a fight, but since it was his girls he made an exception.

The rest of the night went smooth. At the end of the night Sydni counted her tips. Her mind was still on moving, she even thought about asking Mike for the money to move.

She didn't want to give him the wrong impression. But what if he asked her she thought!

Little Eric was over her Mama's house, so it felt good to sleep in the bed alone. It seemed like it had been so long since she had that chance. Lately it was either share the bed with little Eric or with Mike. Sydni had just settled into a deep sleep when the phone rang. She jumped up because it was so late that she automatically assumed that it was an emergency, and it was.

"Sid come get me!" It was Mya on the phone whispering asking for Sydni to help her. "What the...where are you...why are you whispering"? Sydni demanded to know.

"I'm at the house, just come and get me, please"! She hung the phone up in Sydni's ears. Sydni was still groggy from her deep sleep as she got up and quickly put her clothes on.

Mya lived about fifteen minutes from Sydni, but she made it there in half that time breaking every traffic rule. As she pulled up to the house she noticed that all of the lights were out but the door was opened. She reached into her purse and thanked God that Syrus had bought her a little snub nose 38 revolver. As she crept into the house, she heard a whimpering sound coming from the bathroom. Sydni felt fear running through her body. She didn't know what to expect. Here she was walking into the unknown with a gun in her hand and she was ready to use it. When she reached the bathroom and looked in, she almost fainted at what she saw. There was Mya with both eyes swollen and blackened. Her nose was so swollen you couldn't see the bridge. Both lips were busted and swollen and blood trickled out of the side of her mouth.

"Mya, who the hell did this to you"? Sydni was standing over Mya still with the gun in her hand and her finger on the trigger.

37

"Shh! Shh! Please be quiet Sid, he's still here. Just get me out of here". Mya asked as she tried to get up.

"Where is the bastard Mya"? Sydni asked waving the gun in her right hand ready to take him on.

"No Sid please! He'll hurt you"! Mya pleaded.

"Fuck that"! Sydni was past being talked out of confronting Darius. She raised her revolver from her side and stormed into the bedroom where she found Darius passed out on the bed naked. She grabbed the cordless phone and hit him on the side of his head as hard as she could.

"Wake up Bitch"! She hollered standing over him with the phone in one hand and her gun in her other.

Darius jumped up but then he stumbled and fell to the floor. Partly from being drunk, and the rest from the blow that he had received to his head. Sydni kicked him hard in the ribs several times.

"Who the hell do you think you are, Punk? Try beating my ass Motherfucker! Come on get up Punk! You like to beat up on women, beat my ass"!

Darius had planned to do just that as he jumped up, but he changed his mind quickly when he looked into the barrel of her 38 pointed right at his head.

This sudden activity had sobered Darius somewhat to the point that he clearly understood what was going down. "Bitch, you aren't gonna shoot me, you don't even know how to use that little shit you got in your hand." Darius snarled at Sydni. She could see the venom in his eyes. It was clear to her that he had no feeling of remorse for what he had done to Mya.

"Try me Punk! This little shit is big enough to blow your ass away right here and now, and all I need is an excuse, so come try me!

Mya who was watching everything from the doorway begged Sydni not to shoot him.

"Sydni, no......it's not worth it!" Sydni felt hot tears of anger running from her eyes changing to steam as they trickled across her hot face. She knew that she was past the point of reasoning. Mya knew that too, but she kept pleading with Sydni.

"Just let him go Sydni....please"! She grabbed his clothes and threw them at him. "Don't ever come back Darius. This is it... I don't want to ever see you again. Now go. Just leave." Mya stood motionless staring at Darius.

Sydni still had the gun pointed at him as he walked past her. She held the gun in position until he was out of the door. As he was driving off he yelled back.

"Bitch....you should have shot me"!

Sydni was shaking like a leaf as she lowered the gun. At that moment she realized that she would have killed Darius had he made any type of violent move towards her or Mya. It also registered to her that she would have been in serious legal trouble and might have gone to jail. And, what about Little Eric, what would happen to him? Even with all of these thoughts rushing through her mind, she still felt vindicated in coming to her friends rescue. She also knew that if the shoe was on the other foot, Mya would have come to her rescue.

39

"Sid, I am so sorry...I should never have put you in danger".

"I'm not the one in danger Mya. Are you gonna let him kill you? Each time he gets progressively worse, and each time I worry that it will be fatal. Look at your face"!

"I'm afraid, I can feel it all over". Mya said as she started to cry. They sat there for a minute and cried together. It hurt Sydni so bad to see one of her best friends hurt and humiliated. She finally gathered her senses and took her friend to the hospital. Sydni sat in the waiting room the remainder of the night into the wee hours of the morning while they treated Mya. So much for what started as a quiet good night sleep in the comfort of her bed and home.

Sydni called Blake and Ariel and told them of Mya's misfortune. They met at Blake's house for breakfast and discussed in length the horrors of the night before.

"Damn Sid, where did you get that 007 shit from? You've been watching too many movies girl. They all laughed.

"Girl please, I was operating off pure adrenaline and anger at first, afterwards I was scared as hell!" Sydni laughed as she shuddered at the thought that she knew Darius wasn't gone for long, but she didn't bring that up in the conversation. She only hoped that the police caught up with him before he caught up with her! Mya had given a report to the Police at the hospital. They were required to notify the Police when they saw her condition.

"So Mya did you go file a police report? Ariel asked.

Mya still wasn't able to look her friends in the face she was too embarrassed. "The Police came to the hospital. There is a warrant out for his arrest".

"I hope they catch his ass! Seriously Mya, you need to be done with his ass for good." Blake interrupted with her comment. "You know I know how it is to love someone so much that you allow yourself to do dumb things, and you allow dumb things to be done to you. But, you have got to love yourself more. You have to be the most important person in the world to you! We love you and we are going to help you through this. We got your back girl". There wasn't a dry eye in the room after Blake finished talking.

Sydni had agreed to meet Paige at Mama's house around 1:00pm to take her to the mall. They had a lot to discuss. It had been a while since they had gotten together for their sisterly sessions. Rimy and Mama had already left by the time that she arrived. They must have taken Eric with them because he wasn't around either.

When she opened the door she heard sounds coming from the bathroom. "Oh Lord"! Not again she thought as she made her way to the bathroom. Sydni was relieved when she found Paige slouched over the toilet throwing up her breakfast.

"Sid...I can't do it. This is killing me. My stomach muscles hurt, my throat is sore and I can't keep anything down".

"So Paige, maybe we shouldn't go to the mall, maybe we should just stay here and talk".

"Okay Sid, I just want to go back and lie down". Paige was grateful for Sydni's compassion. They went downstairs to her lair in the basement. Paige's bed was neatly decorated with "Hello Kitty" spreads with matching everything from valances to the stationary on her desk. Everything matched perfectly. Sydni felt awkward sitting on her neatly made bed. Paige was so goody-goody that it made Sydni sick.

"So what's it gonna be kiddo"? Sydni asked.

"I talked to Zo, and he is pretty neutral about it. He says he will support me either way. I just don't know if I'm ready for this." Paige looked like she could cry any minute. As Sydni looked around the room, she realized that Paige was still a kid. She also knew that even though she was very mature for her age, she was not ready to raise a child.

"Paige, I know that you love Zo, but I want you to take a minute and remember how hard it was for me when Eric was born. There is no more me- me- me-. It's the baby first. You won't like using your last ten dollars to pay for some diapers, but you will. You will have to sacrifice a lot, like going out with your friends. You can't go unless you can find a sitter, and will you have the money to pay a sitter, if it is not a family member? Now you know Rimy and myself, we have your back. But, try going out and just getting home, and the baby isn't ready to go back to sleep, so you have to stay up until he or she is ready to go to sleep. It's not easy having someone depend on you for everything. It's not easy at all. You need to consider all of this before you make your mind up. I love Eric, but sometimes I wish I could've waited just a little while longer".

"Sid, I don't want to keep the baby; will you help me do what I have to do"?

"You know I will kid". Sydni hugged her little sister tight kissing her on the cheek. She seemed so small again, she thought to herself.

I have got to get some sleep or I will not be able to work tonight, Sydni thought as she pulled in front of her house. When she walked in there was a note from her father asking her to clean up the bathroom when she got a chance. She was furious as she slung the note on the floor. "Who else is going to do it, Eric"? She questioned what her dad was thinking when he wrote the note. Just then she heard her phone ringing upstairs. "Hello" she said out of breath as she grabbed the phone after running up the stairs.

"What's up baby"? It was Mike.

"I'm just pissed off with my dad. He hasn't said anything about moving and he is treating me like I'm a damn kid. I don't know what I'm going to do".

"Why don't you move baby"? Mike asked sympathetically.

Here's my chance Sydni thought. "How am I suppose to do that? I don't have anything in my savings and the bar is slowing down". She paused to dramatize her point.

"Well find a place and I'll give you what you need". Mike said.

"No Mike, you have given me so much already, I'll just try to stick it out here". Sydni stated with a smirk on her face, waiting for Mike to over-rule her feeble attempt at being independent.

"Hell naw, if you don't have to suffer. Why would you want to"? Mike countered.

"I'm just saying". Mike cut Sydni off. "No Sydni I'm just saying find a place. By the way---where were you last night? I called about three and you didn't answer the phone."

Sydni thought twice about telling the truth, but decided against it. "I was sleep, I had a rough night at the bar". At least it was part of the truth.

Sydni set out to find her an apartment pronto. After looking around at a few places, she settled on a townhouse in a suburb right outside of the city. Not too close and not too far. Mike took her to Art Van and let her pick out all new furniture for the apartment. After everything was purchased, she figured he had gone through at least $17,000. She was thoroughly impressed with this brother. Eric loved his new house and she was extremely happy. Mike would only come over a few nights out of the week, which was also good for Sydni, that way she didn't feel crowded.

Her first disagreement with Mike came after she had asked him to pick up Eric from daycare and had given him her extra set of keys. Absent-mindedly she forgot to retrieve them from him. She was shocked shitless one day when she came home and found Mike and his friends sitting in her living room smoking weed and drinking beer.

"Hey baby". Mike said as she opened the door. She could feel her face getting beet red by the seconds as she surveyed the room.

"Get your damn feet off my table Negro"! She yelled at one of his friends as he scrambled to straighten up. "Mike I need to see you upstairs". She said as she stared the friends down.

When Sydni got upstairs she lit right into Mike. "How dare you enter my house and bring your low-life friends where my son lays his head"!

"Whoa! Did I hear you say your house"? Mike asked with an attitude.

44

"Yes, you did hear me, I said –my house." Sydni didn't back down.

"What bills have you paid Sydni? Did you forget who put you in this house? I pay the bills and if I want to come here when you aren't here, I can. Yeah…dog was wrong for having his feet on the table, but you handled that. I don't want to ever hear that (my house) shit again. This is our house. Is that clear"?

Sydni couldn't say anything she recognized that basically everything that he had said was true. He was responsible for everything in the place as well as the place. She just stood there and watched him turn around and go downstairs and continue to entertain his company. She was sure that he had gone downstairs and showed the fellas how he handled his business in putting his woman in check.

It was the first time he had ever raised his voice at her, not to mention saying the things to her that he did. She was reeling in shock as she sat down on her $2500 pillow top mattress and cried.

Two weeks had passed since Mike and Sydni's encounter. She realized that she had over- reacted, but only in the sense that the man was her benefactor and without what he had done for her, she might have been at home with her dad dealing with the same old shit that she was living with. She was ready to apologize by the time that he came by. He surprised her by bringing her an anklet made with white gold X's and diamond O's. He also bought her a black Versace pants suit and a pair of Via Spiga boots from Saks. They both apologized and made up. Sydni was again riding high and feeling good.

Shawntel had called and invited Sydni to a party at Club Blue, a popular club downtown. Sydni had a babysitter and hadn't been out for a while, so she decided to join her friend for a drink.

Her girlfriend Shawntel was definitely "model material" she was about 5'9" and very slim. Her beautiful long straight hair, flowing down her back embraced her copper complexion. And it was hers. The two of them were getting plenty of attention.

Sydni was standing at the bar trying to order a drink when a tall gentleman walked up beside her and asked if he could buy her a drink. Sydni hadn't taken a close look at him, she was more focused on getting her drink and returning to her table. Her comment to the gentleman was, "good luck, maybe you'll have better luck than I am". Sydni smiled as she watch the busy barmaid work.

"Mika, get shortie whatever she is drinking and put it on my tab".

Right away Mika waltzed right over and took Sydni's order. Syd was impressed with his power of persuasion. Sydni thanked the man for the drink. It was at this time that she finally focused on the man himself and what she saw wasn't bad at all. He told her his name was Kevin. He stood about 6'5" and had a muscular build, perfectly groomed beard, and beautiful straight teeth. He definitely had it going on and he had her attention, but she was cool.

"You're welcome, it's not a problem." He was responding to Sydni's thanking him for the drink. "My name is Kevin and my friends and I are giving this party".

"Well, I appreciate you getting my drink, cause Sistah is humping back there and I know how she feels". Sydni answered.

"Are you a bartender"? He asked.

"Yes, at Club On The Mile". She answered.

"Well, I'm gonna have to come check out your Long Islands one day". Kevin mused.

"One day soon I hope". Sydni answered.

"Do you have a phone number I can call you at"? He asked. That's when the dream that she was in faded and she snapped back into reality. She knew that she couldn't give him her phone number as bad as she wanted to. So, she settled on giving him her pager and cell phone numbers.

"Save me a dance beautiful.....all right? Don't forget me." He smiled as he walked away.

"Girl who was that? He is fine as hell!" Shawntel replied shaking her head wishing it was her who he had hit on. "I know I love him already." Sydni said. She didn't see Kevin anymore until the end of the night. He promised to give her a call soon.

It was that time. The next morning Sydni and Paige went to the "Women's Clinic". She signed Paige in while she paced back and forth.

"Calm down sis, it's gonna be okay. Are you 100% sure that this is what you want to do? Because it's not too late, we can walk right out the door right now." Deep down inside Sydni hoped and prayed that it was because they had already waited as long as they could. She had reached the limit because the doctors wouldn't perform the abortion after sixteen weeks.

"Sydni, I'm sure that this is what I want to do. I'm just scared that it will hurt"! Paige looked at Sydni and waited for a consoling word.

"Well, it might hurt a little, but it will be over in less than ten minutes." Sydni said, as she picked up some pamphlets and began to read about the procedure that would be performed on her sister in a few minutes. Paige's name was called by the medical technician. Paige turned around and waved just before she left the waiting room and walked into the operating room. Sydni said a silent prayer in hopes that her sister had made the right decision and that she would be okay both physically and mentally.

Three hours later a groggy Paige woke Sydni up. She had nodded off while waiting. "Damn what took you so long? I thought it only took ten minutes? Sydni asked Paige.

"I had to go to a counseling session to make sure this was what I wanted to do. Then the procedure was done. It actually took twenty minutes for them to prep me and the actual procedure took only ten minutes. Then I had to stay in the recovery room for an hour. I have to go get these prescriptions filled and then I want to go to bed." Paige was yawning as she spoke.

CHAPTER 4

"So did it hurt"? Sydni asked – "Yeah, a little. It was like severe menstrual cramps. It definitely wasn't as bad as I imagined it would be. I probably feel worse mentally". Paige was tired and emotionally whipped.

"I'm sorry that you had to go through this, but I'm pretty sure it's the best thing for you". With gentle care, Sydni pulled her sister close and gave her an understanding supportive hug. "You are straight breaking me today though. You can't use your medical card to fill those prescriptions either, or Mama will know. So I guess I have to pay cash for those too".

"I already know I owe you a lot". Paige took a deep breath and let it out slowly, as if asking herself. "How did I get into this mess"?

"Yeah, but don't worry about it, we'll negotiate later. Let's get home". As Sydni backed out of the parking space she could feel her sister's eyes on her.

"What?" Sydni asked.

"Nothing, I just love you". Paige couldn't hold those words any longer.

"I love you too. I know that you already know that". Sydni answered back.

By the time that Sydni arrived at her house, she was disappointed to see Mike had come home, she didn't expect him. He hadn't been there in three days and she was happy about it. Their relationship had changed drastically. He was constantly reminding her that he paid the bills and that she should be grateful of that. The sex had become boring as hell and it was getting harder and harder for her to fake it. Besides, it wasn't fun feeling like a possession rather than a woman free to love and be loved by her man with no reservations or threats.

Just as Sydni and Paige walked into the house the phone began ringing. Paige went to answer it. Sydni walked past Mike without so much as a smile.

"What's wrong now"? He asked.

"Where have you been for three days"? Sydni asked pretending to really care.

"Don't even start that shit! You know I have to take care of business, no matter how long it takes. Don't forget.....I pay the bills'.

'I know you pay the bills...you never let me forget"! With that she walked upstairs to get a bed ready for Paige. She cooled out getting some well needed rest and slept all night without a whimper.

Sydni had promised Eric that they would go to the movies the next day and she knew he was pumped. She had to be careful what you promised him. It was almost better to tell him at the last minute because he would drive her crazy asking about the event. Mama had him dressed and ready when she got there.

"Hey Mommy. Are you ready for the movies"? He asked jumping up and down excited and ready to go. Eric looked so cute in his Tommy Hilfiger coverall and matching T-shirt.

Mike had just bought him the newly released Air Jordan's and a new Tommy coat to match.

"Yes baby.....Mommy is ready".

Mama had that quizzical look on her face. "Where's Paige? I thought she spent the night over your house." Mama asked.

"She did Mama, she was still sleep, so I didn't wake her". Sydni has just told a (Peace Lie). That is a lie told specifically to keep the peace.

"Have you talked to her yet? I swear I think she is pregnant." Mama stated as she buttoned up Eric's coat.

"She's not pregnant Mama". (At least that part was true now) "She just had something on her mind, school and Zo mainly. Come on E. let's go". She couldn't stand lying to her mother like that, but she thought it best. "Mama I'll call you later, we are meeting Ariel and Isis at the theater".

The Movie Theater was jammed packed with little kids dying to see "Monster's Inc.". Sydni and Eric made their way through the crowd to the designated spot where she was to meet Ariel and Isis. She was surprised to see them already there.

"I thought I was early, it is too damn crowded in here so I already bought the tickets. You can get the refreshments." Sydni told Ariel.

"That's cool". Ariel stated.

It felt like they were in a sea of midgets as they swam through the crowd to the refreshment stand. Ariel had stopped to talk to some guy. Eric and Isis were following

51

Sydni, when they finally reached the stand she looked down and asked them what they wanted. They both agreed on popcorn and Sour Patch kids, they agreed to split a Hawaiian punch. Sydni let go of their hands momentarily to get money out of her purse to pay for the refreshments. When she reached back down only one hand grabbed hers, it was Eric. Isis was no where to be found! Frantically Sydni looked around the general vicinity of the stand. She then looked over to where Ariel was standing still talking and she wasn't with her either. Sydni's heart was pounding rapidly and in her stomach.

As Sydni approached Ariel she noticed the frightened look on her face. She also saw that Isis wasn't with her.

"Where is Isis"? Ariel asked frantically.

"Ariel she was standing right here a minute ago. I let her hand go long enough to reach into my purse to get money for the refreshments and when I reached back for her she was gone"!

"Oh my God! My Baby! Sydni help me find her." They both searched frantically stopping everyone that they passed by asking if they had seen this little girl. It was only minutes, but it seemed like hours. They asked the Security Guard to issue an alert. Ariel was trying to stay calm and doing a pretty good job of it. Sydni on the other hand was a nervous wreck. Probably because Isis was left in her charge and she felt responsible. Isis was her godchild it was like losing her own child.

Suddenly Eric started pulling her hand trying to get away. "Stop Eric, stand still." Sydni demanded yelling at Eric. He began to cry.

"What's wrong baby? Ariel asked Eric. "I want to go over there with Icy." He cried out. They looked over to where he was pointing. There she was curled up in a drag racing video game sleep. A flood of relief fell over both women. Ariel finally let out, she had been calm and cool, but she was outwardly crying tears of joy now. She ran over and picked up her sleeping child from her hiding place. After the movie was over, Sydni vowed to herself that it would be a long time before they came back to the theater.

When Sydni got back to her home Paige was up watching TV. She looked at her and sized her up. The rest had done her good. "How are you doing?" Sydni asked Paige.

"I'm okay, just hungry!" Paige answered.

Sydni was glad to hear that she was handling the situation so well, and that she had her appetite.

"Do you mind if Zo comes over and sit with me for a minute"?

"No baby, I don't care. He can come over. Is he bringing you something to eat"? Sydni asked.

"He said he was". Paige answered.

"Well lay back down, I'm going to clean up and wash some clothes. Don't let Eric get on your nerves.

"He wont, he loves his auntie." Paige said as she pulled him up in the bed with her and hugged him. Eric squealed with delight.

Sydni's pager suddenly went off. She looked but didn't recognize the number. She called back and ask. "Did someone call a pager from there"? A deep voice answered. "Yes, this is Kevin. Is this Sydni"?

"Yes it is. What's up with you"? She was excited to hear his voice.

"Just checking to make sure you gave me the right number, you know how you ladies do sometimes. I noticed you didn't give me your home phone number. I assume you have a situation." Kevin asked trying to get his bearings.

"Your assumptions are correct and I don't want to give you the spill about how we aren't getting along. Everyone uses that line. Even though it is true in my case". She said.

"Well if it's true in your case, then I can count on hearing from you again then....right"? He asked.

"Yeah, I think you can, but I'm at home right now so I'll call you back later." Sydni hung the phone up grinning from ear to ear. She then proceeded to wash her load of clothes.

The weeks seemed to fly by. It was already the middle of December and you could definitely tell it was going to be one cold winter. Sydni was headed to the airport to pick her cousin Chelsea. Master P's "How you do dat there" was jamming on the radio and Sydni was bobbing her head as she cruised along. In the mist of this her cell phone rang. "Hello"! She answered.

"What's up boo"? It was Mike. "Same O..Same O. What's up with you"? Sydni asked.

"I wanted to know if you have enough money to pick up the food for your party"? Mike asked.

Sydni had more than enough money, she hadn't paid a bill in three months, and she hadn't made it to the mall yet.

"No I don't, I was waiting on you to get back". Where are you anyway? I thought you were coming back yesterday." It must be something up there other than some money that keeps you there all the time. Don't tell me you are giving my shit away." Sydni was laughing to herself and faking like she was vomiting. About that time a little old White lady pulled up besides her and shook her head in disgust. Of course Sydni gave her the "finger".

"Now you know I'm not doing anybody else, I can barely keep up with you". Mike replied.

"You got that right. Well, I'm picking Chelsea up from the airport now, so what do you want me to do? She asked. "I'll pick up the food when I get down there. I'm on the freeway now". Mike told Sydni.

"You are too sweet....bye baby". Sydni answered and hung up the phone   Sydni pulled into the visitor's lot of the metro airport. She rode around for a minute until she spotted a family walking slowly towards a parked car. She decided to wait for their space. The mother had to be at least 300 pounds and her three little kids were half her size. This was disgusting to Sydni and she wondered how she could let her kids get so big. Eric would be on a diet so fast, that it would make your head spin, she thought. It took the lady about ten minutes to get to her car and put the suitcases and her fat little kids in. She took another two minutes to stuff her fat ass in. And two more minutes to navigate the big boat of a car that she was driving out of the space. Just then right in front of her eyes another car whipped around the corner and whipped into the space that she had been waiting fifteen minutes for. It was the same old lady she had given the finger to on the freeway.

"Oh hell naw"! Sydni jumped out of her car and went over to the old lady's car and politely stated her views.

"Ma'am, I been waiting on this space for over ten minutes. How do you think you can just round the corner and take my space?

The old lady opened her door, grabbed her cane, got out and closed her door. She acted as if Sydni wasn't even there.

"Excuse me...did you hear what I said, are you deaf or something"? She asked. Just then Chelsea came walking up and stated.

"Girl, leave that lady alone!

The lady was ignoring Sydni anyway and had basically turned her back and walked away. That is, after Sydni had jumped in front of her and informed her that she was a rude ass old lady, and if she were twenty years younger she would have kicked her ass. The lady reached for her ear and said.

"I'm sorry....I didn't have my hearing aid turned on. Did you say something young lady"? The old lady asked.

Chelsea replied for Sydni: "No ma'am, have a good day".

The lady turned and walked away and chuckled to herself, "that will teach her to give me the finger!

Sydni stomped back to her car and threw Chelsea's bags in the back. "Hey be careful with that. That is Louis Vuitton!" Chelsea screamed.

"You could have carried it yourself, I peeped that Louis flavor though. Sean must be high on the hog right about now! Sydni teased her cousin.

"Yeah, we're doing alright, I just can't get with the sex. I've tried everything. He thinks I'm a freak......I'm just trying to get off. The size of the ship does matter especially if he doesn't have the motion in the ocean". Chelsea spoke choosing her words carefully. "I am sexually frustrated too"! Said Sydni

"You haven't cheated"! Chelsea asked Sydni.

"Not yet but I swear I'm tempted to do some backtracking. You know big Eric might be a loser but he was a champion in the bedroom! Sydni set the record straight laughing.

"You know you are crazy, don't you? Chelsea asked. Chelsea loved her cousin. They had spent every summer of their childhood together down in their home state of Illinois. Sydni, Rimy and Paige would stay with her and her mom. They would drive her mom crazy! Chelsea was estatic when Paige told her that they were giving a party for Sydni. It gave her a chance to get away from her problems at home.

Her plan was to not think about Sean while she was there. She came to have a good time and chill with some Detroit ballers and shotcallers.

Her cousin Sydni always showed her a good time when she came up.

Mike had already made it back to the house by the time that they got there. Chelsea went over and gave Mike a big hug she then scooped up Eric and proceeded to give him her un-divided attention. Mike had picked him up from daycare.

"Damn baby, you must have been closer than you said, since you had enough time to pick up E."? Sydni asked.

"Yeah...you don't ever know where I might pop up"! Mike spouted off with a smirk.

"What's that suppose to mean? You stalking me now"? Sydni asked. Not too happy with his comment.

"No, I'm just playing girl. There's the food, when is your Mama coming to cook"? Mike asked.

"Tomorrow afternoon, I have to work tonight. So, Chelsea are you hanging at the bar with me?" Sydni answered Mike's question and asked her own of Chelsea.

"For sure". Chelsea repled.

"I have to go make some runs, I'll get with y'all later". Mike was leaving the group when Eric started crying because he wanted to go with him. "Little Man you can't go with me, but when I come back I'm gonna bring you something....okay"? That sounded like a bargain to Eric. He wiped his face and nodded his head. He loved new toys or gym shoes.

"You are spoiling him, you know that right"? Sydni asked Mike.

"Look who's talking, you've got a lot of nerve making that statement". He laughed. "I set some money on the dresser for you to get something to wear. Now is everybody happy? Can I go now"?

"Yes, and thank you baby. Bye boy!" Sydni smiled and waved to him goodbye.

It was Sydni's birthday and certainly a night that she wanted to work at the bar. With her popularity she was sure to receive a nice piece of change.

The DJ kept announcing it over the mike that it was Sydni's birthday. Each time that he did, everyone would yell and clap for her. They started pinning money on her shirt and by the end of the night she had well over $1000 on her shirt. She was having the time of her life. Even Mya had come out, she had been keeping a low profile lately. Tonight she seemed to be her old self again. She was really looking cute in her Donna Karan stretch outfit. Mya's "ghetto" booty always attracted the guys. Sydni was really happy to see that physically she was healing, she wasn't too sure about her mental healing.

Her other girl friends were too, but they were working. Blake was looking good, she had started taking her diet pills and exercising. She looked slimmer, like some of the weight was dropping off and that meant a lot to Blake. She seemed happier as she ran around the bar like a Tasmanian devil serving drinks.

By the end of the night Chelsea was tucked off in a corner getting her talk on with this fine young man. Everyone was cleaning up when Sydni noticed Blake swaying and stumbling as she walked. She looked like she was drunk or something.

"Hey Blake! Did you drink some of what you served tonight? Sydni asked. When Blake turned around, she stumbled again and Sydni noticed that she was sweating profusely.

"Hey girl---are you alright? Why are you sweating so bad?" Sydni asked.

Blake laughed nervously and stated: "This is part of the program. I'm suppose to sweat off the inches".

"I'm sorry Boo, but you look a little funny to me, go ahead and sit down. I'll finish the floor". Ariel told her sick friend.

Blake gladly accepted her offer and sat down. She was afraid to admit to her friends that she was feeling funny, and had been for a few days.

"Chelsea, do you think you could wrap up that conversation? I'm ready to go. Sydni said to her cousin.

"My bad! Vaughn let me introduce you to my cousin. This is Sydni. Sydni, this Vaughan!

"I know Vaughn. Aren't you a friend of Mike's"? Sydni asked.

"Yeah, I thought you looked familiar". He said.

"I invited him to the party tomorrow, is that alright Sydni?" Chelsea asked.

"Yeah that's okay. Then I guess we will see you then". Sydni stated to Vaughn.

"Well, Vaughn and I are going for coffee, so I will meet you back at the house in a little while".

Sydni, Blake, and Ariel all said, "hmmm-mm!"

"Shut up y'all! I'm a grown ass woman." Chelsea reminded them.

"Vaughn bring my cousin back in one piece, you hear me"? Sydni warned him.

"For sure". He said as they left.

Mike was already home waiting for Sydni when she got there. He wanted to know why it had taken her so long to get home.

"What, am I being timed now? She asked.

"Look, I just asked a question. Why are you always on the defensive"?

"Because I have to be this way with you. The same way you always have to remind me who is in charge"! She answered back.

"Well Sydni, you go out and try to make the money I make and pay all the bills, and then you will be in charge. You ungrateful bitch"!

"What did you just call me?" She asked.

"I called you an ungrateful bitch! There's a thousand hoes out there dying to be in your shoes, and you are always complaining about something". Mike said.

"You bastard, you will not disrespect me like that. You can get the hell out of my house. I'll show your ass that I can pay my own damn bills. You act like you are the only brotha out here making money. Did you forget who my ex-boyfriend is? You haven't did shit that the next brotha won't do. Brothas like you come a dime a dozen. You won't be hard to replace." With that she turned to walk away having thoroughly reduced him to his lowest common denominator. He grabbed her by her neck and pushed her against the wall.

She could feel the anger that she had stirred up in him pulsing through his veins as he tightened his grip around her neck. His breath was hot on her face as he told her.

"I will beat your ass if you even think about another brotha......you understand me"?

Sydni could barely breathe let alone answer him, but she managed to nod her head. All the while she was thinking, "as soon as this punk let's me go, I'm gonna kill his ass".

At that moment she heard padded footsteps as Eric came in their bedroom and climbed in the bed. Mike let her go before Eric could see what he had been doing. Sydni glared at Mike as she scooped Eric up and walked out of the room. She was physically and mentally upset. She decided that she would sleep in Eric's room that night to keep herself from doing something that she might regret. Later on that night Mike crept into Eric's room and woke Sydni up.

"Baby, I'm sorry, I know I shouldn't have put my hands on you but, you made me so mad. I love you so much and I don't want to lose you. Come back to our bed, please"!

Sydni got up and went back. Deep down she knew that Mike was not a violent guy, and that maybe she had been complaining a lot lately. He does so much for me and Eric, maybe I should just go easy on him, she thought.

Once they were in bed, Mike began to massage her shoulders and back. He then turned her over and kissed her neck and traced circles around her breasts. Moving very slowly down to her stomach, he softly kissed her naval. She was feeling really good now, as she parted her legs and welcomed his eager tongue guiding it to her warm spot. She moved her hips and helped him bring her to a climax. Sydni moaned as the warm currents floated through her body. She jumped on top of him and placed him inside of her and began to ride him. Before she knew it she was envisioning herself on top of Kevin. Sydni pinched his nipples as she moved aggressively, yearning for her next orgasm. She felt him reach up and grab her breasts but Sydni was in another world, it was Kevin who was grabbing her breast and coaxing her next orgasm. It was Kevin who laid her down and plunged inside of her and satisfied himself with little help from her. Sydni snapped back into reality when Mike fell out on top of her and nearly knocked the wind out of her. As he rolled over and instantly started to snore, Sydni thought to herself. "Thank you Kevin!"

The next morning Sydni woke up to Eric pulling her eyelids open. "Mommy wake up, it's your birthday!" Eric screamed. "Happy birthday Mama! Go Mama it's your birthday! Go Mama it's your birthday"!

"Thank you baby"! Sydni hugged Eric. "Mama can I come to your party"? Eric asked.

"Eric honey, my party tonight is for grown ups, but tomorrow grandma is giving me ice cream and cake and I want you to help me cut my cake"!

"Yeah Mama I want to cut your cake"! He mused.

At that point Sydni realized that Chelsea hadn't made it home from the night before. "Mike get up! Vaughn did not bring Chelsea home last night! Page him"! She pleaded.

"Sydni, Chelsea is grown." Mike yawned and sat in silence while he found his bearings after waking up. "Did you ever stop to think that she didn't want to come home last night? I know Vaughn hasn't done anything to that girl". He said.

"Well you can still call him to make sure.....please"! Sydni pleaded.

Mike got up to make the call, and then the doorbell rang. Sydni ran downstairs to answer it. In walks Chelsea all sunny and bright, bubbling all over. Sydni wasn't bubbling.

"Where the hell you been"? Sydni asked.

"Once again Sydni......I am grown. You do not have to worry about me." Chelsea responded as she kicked off her shoes.

"Yeah Chelsea...you are grown, but I do have to worry about you. If anything were to happen to you while you're here visiting me, I would never be able to forgive myself, even though you are grown. Chelsea you didn't even know that boy"! Sydni declared.

"O.K., but when did you get all righteous and pure? Besides I know him a lot better today! I need a shower; can you get me a washcloth and a towel"? Chelsea asked.

Sydni couldn't say anything more she just looked at her and laughed. Chelsea was always the rebellious type. Being the only child hadn't helped in that department.

"I have to go to the mall to find something to wear tonight. Are you coming"? "I am Eric answered". "I know you are silly, I'm talking to Chelsea". Sydni replied.

"Yes, I'm coming." Chelsea stated.

"So everybody be ready in like thirty minutes". Sydni told her group.

The mall was jammed pack. The Christmas shopping season had started two weeks before but it didn't seemed to make a difference with the crowd, it seemed to be just as busy. Mya had agreed to meet them there. After they found her they then went into Chelsea's favorite store Bebe's. Sydni and Mya watched as Chelsea modeled clothes. They both agreed that Chelsea looked good in a pair of brown leather pants with a blouse that had brown, beige, orange and burgundy swirls on it. She bought the outfit and they left going into Neimans. Here, Sydni picked out a black knee length skirt by Dolce and Gabbana, and a black fitted sweater. She had already bought riding boots from Nine West that had a 4 inch heel. I am going be banging with this outfit she stated to the group. Mya was deciding on a black or brown suede skirt. After she picked out her outfit, they ventured into the shoe and purse section.

"It feels so good to shop. It's been too long." Mya reminded her crew. "Not long enough for me. Sean is going to trip when he sees these bags". Chelsea stated.

"That's the one thing that I can say about Mike, he always wants me to look good. So, shopping is o.k.." Sydni exclaimed.

"Girl, you got it made". Mya stated.

After they had each successfully picked out the sharpest outfits that they could find, Mya left to take little Darius to the dentist. She was cautioned not to be late by Sydni. Mya yelled over her shoulders as she left stating that she wouldn't.

"So what's next"? Do you want to get something to eat"? Chelsea asked.

"I want McDonalds". Eric blurted.

"Well we can get you Mickey D's, and then we're going to Outback Steakhouse". Sydni replied.

It had been a pleasant experience shopping for the girls, and a good time just being out with the kids. Now it was party time. Sydni's house was jammed packed with people. Mama was in the kitchen cooking. Paige and Rimy had just gotten back from dropping Eric off and were decorating the apartment. Chelsea was showering downstairs and Sydni upstairs. Ariel was helping Mama when her jam came on.

"Hey—that's my jam". Mama said. "Come on y'all. Gonna have a funky good time, gonna have a funky good time". Mama was singing her heart out and having a good time. All the girls lined up and started doing the hustle to that song.

"Mama you are too stiff, loosen up some". Rimy said. They all laughed. Sydni came downstairs in her bathrobe and joined in. They were cracking up over Mama she looked just like one of them! Even at 47 years old, she could easily pass for 21. Mama always complained that her girls dressed her too young, but it was hard to buy for someone so petite. She was too little for the misses department, so the girls bought her clothes from the juniors department. There had been times when Sydni and Mama would be out together and young guys would be trying to hit on Mama just as much as they were hitting on Sydni. Blake told Sydni to take her ass upstairs and get dressed before the guest started to arrive. She expected that to happen soon.

"Okay I'm going. I'm scared of you Blake. Don't be trying to out shine me at my own party." Sydni laughed as she cracked on Blake. Blake had on a black prada pants suit and some bad- ass boots.

"Shut up Sydni"! Blake stated to her as she ran upstairs to get dressed.

Second Time ... Shame On Me.

CHAPTER 5

Everyone seemed to be enjoying themselves at the party. Mike had hired a bartender for the night and they had enough liquor for at least 100 people. He made sure Mama had her Absolut and orange juice. Champagne was flowing like Niagra Falls. Sydni was loving life, she gave Mike a gentle kiss of appreciation and thanked him for a hell of a party. Chelsea was dancing with Vaughn and looking like a woman in love. Shawntel had just showed up with her husband John.

"Hey Boo! Said Sydni as she kissed John and took their coats. She sent them over to the bar to get their drinks. At that point Ariel announced that it was time to open up the gifts. Everyone gathered around Sydni as she began opening her gifts. She got a lot of cards with money in them. Mama had bought her a really nice cashmere hat and scarf set. Mya bought her a red Coach purse. Blake and Ariel went in together and got her a $300 gift certificate to Dolce Vita. Shawntel had bought her some beautiful diamond cut gold hoop earrings. Finally she got to Mike's gift, which was hanging in the closet. She knew what it was as soon as she saw the Dittrich's bag. He had bought her a blue diamond mink coat, with matching hat and muff. Everyone gasped and began to clap when they saw it. All of her friends were slapping her on the back and giving her high fives. Mike had a huge smile on his face he knew that he had brought the maximum happiness out of her at that moment. He really liked to see Sydni deliriously happy. Mike walked up to her and gave her a jewelry box. Everyone quieted down and waited with baited breath as she opened the box. Inside was a 3-carat tennis bracelet. It was awesome! This was definitely the best birthday that she had ever had. After she finished opening her gifts everyone went back to dancing. By the end of the night Sydni was so drunk she passed out.

Sydni woke up the next morning with a splitting headache. She had cottonmouth so bad she was dying for a glass of water. When she got up she realized that she was naked! She could only imagine what had gone on after she passed out. Mike was still sleeping, so she climbed over him and found her robe.

Sydni held her head with one hand, and the stair railing with the other as she went down stairs. When she got there she found Blake asleep on the couch, Mya and Ariel were on the floor. She remembered that Chelsea had left with Vaughn. There was a guy that she did not know sleep with his head down on the dining room table. She padded over to the kitchen and poured herself a glass of water. She ended up drinking three glasses before she realized it.

"What a party"! Sydni thought as she went into the living room to try and wake up her friends. She didn't have any luck there, so she went back up stairs and back to sleep.

The next time that Sydni woke up everyone was gone and her house looked normal again. The girls had cleaned up before they left. Sydni still had her splitting headache. She heard Chelsea moving around in Eric's bedroom. She was packing her bags in preparation for her return trip back home.

"What's the hurry"? Sydni asked.

"I forgot I had an early flight back. My flight leaves in an hour and fifteen minutes".
"Damn! Do I have to take you"? Sydni asked.

"No asshole your Mama is gonna take me". "Where is Vaughn"? Sydni asked.

"Girl, you will never guess what that dumb ass did last night!

"What"? Sydni asked.

"This fool answered my cell phone and it was Sean. I blamed it on Mike, but he didn't buy it, he didn't think that it was Mike. So he's tripping about now". Chelsea's voice trailed as she sighed.

"Are you gonna be alright? Sydni asked.

"I guess so shit! I have caught him doing plenty of shit. But, don't call my house today, because he is mad at you too."

"Why? I didn't do anything". Sydni asked.

"You know how Mike thinks that I be hooking you up when you come down there with me. It's the same with Sean".

"Tell his ass, I didn't have anything to do with that". Sydni directed Chelsea to take care of that.

Just then they heard the horn honking outside. "Well Boobe have a safe flight back and call me when you get there". Chelsea smiled at Sydni. She was the only person who still used her childhood nickname.

"I will". "Be careful wearing that fur around the –D-". "You know I will". Sydni yelled out the door to Mama.

"What are you cooking today Mama"?

"Nothing, eat some of those leftovers you have from the party". Mama yelled back. "Aww ma! Come on now!" Sydni whined.

"Aw Ma my ass, I'm not cooking, you either eat what you got, or you're gonna be hungry". Sydni watched as Mama drove off. "Man, let me get up and go get my baby".

Sydni has been contemplating on getting another job, particularly since she had run into an old colleague who had offered her a job as an office manager of a Micobrewery in the downtown area.   It was Monday the day of her appointment, so after dropping Eric off at daycare she went and met with Marc Hamilton, president of the company. The meeting took place at a small coffee shop in Greektown. Mark was nothing like she imagined. He was maybe ten years older than she was and very casual. He had jeans and a plaid shirt with a sports coat on. They discussed the job and the benefit package. He seemed very impressed with Sydni's skills.   She had worked 3 years as the office manager at a law firm where she had met the colleague who had offered this job. Sydni felt that the interview had gone well and decided that she wanted the job.

Mike had gone on another of his out of town trips. Sydni took Eric with her to the grocery store, there was a huge winter storm brewing so she felt that she had better stock up on goodies for Eric and herself. As she walked down the isles shopping, she felt a little itch on her vagina. She thought maybe her panties were too tight, or that she had been sweating. She decided to ignore it, and didn't feel it again until she got home. Sydni went into the bathroom and pulled down her jogging pants and looked through her pubic hair. She was looking for a hair bump or something that would justify the itch. What she found almost sent her to the floor. She had crabs! Sydni was devastated she had never

72

experienced anything like this before. Her first thought was to call Mama.

"Calm down Sydni, it's okay, you're not gonna die". Mama was always a calming factor for Sydni. "I'll be over in a minute, okay"?

"Mama hurry.... Please"! Sydni hated bugs anyway, and to see them on her body was more than she could deal with calmly. The fifteen minutes that it took Mama get there seemed like the worst fifteen minutes of her life.

"Have you called him yet"? Mama asked.

"Yes, but he isn't answering his cell phone. Mama, you know that this is it! I knew his ass was cheating. His dirty ass! He didn't even have enough respect to cheat with a decent girl. What if he didn't use a condom? I swear I am going to kick his ass Mama. I can't believe this shit"! Sydni screamed loudly.

Mama pulled out a small bottle of lotion called "Rid". Sydni was grossed out, but she showered and used the lotion. By that time Mama had put Eric to sleep and stripped down her bed.

"You need to throw all this away and any of your unclean underwear". Mama told Sydni.

"Mama I feel so dirty.....how could he do this to me"? She was still in her robe as Mama reached down and hugged her as she sat on her bed. She thanked God for Mama.

Sydni paged Mike all night and called his cell phone, but she was unable to make contact with him. The next morning he came in while she was asleep. He was standing over her when she woke up. Sydni lashed out at him calling him everything but a child of God. She asked him how he could be so trifling.

"Did you use a condom Mike? Is there anything else I'm gonna pop up with you bastard? You didn't even have the balls to tell me. I know your nasty ass had to be itching too. I'm leaving your ass! You didn't even have enough respect to sleep with a clean bitch. You chose the nastiest Hoe you could find and put my life in her hands. Mike did you stop to think that if she has crabs, what else she might have? I guess I can answer that myself.....you didn't think! You didn't even give a damn about Eric. He gets up in this bed all the time. I hate your ass, just stay away from me Mike".

Mike was speechless, there was nothing that he could say, he had fucked up and he was busted.

Sydni picked up a newspaper that same day and began looking for another apartment.

After getting busted Mike decided he was going to try and right his wrong. This wasn't going to be easy with Sydni not speaking to him. If he walked into a room, she would immediately leave the room. She had started sleeping in Eric's room. He had flowers sent to her job everyday. She wasn't impressed though.

Sydni and Kris Valentine, the CEO of Microbrewery had become very good friends. He noticed all of the flowers that she was receiving and asked her if something was wrong.

"Hey, did someone die? What's with the flowers"? He asked.

Sydni was looking in the classified ads for a place.

74

"Gosh, you just started! Are you looking for another job already? Kris asked.

"I'm sorry Kris; I'm looking for an apartment. The flowers are from my ex-boyfriend." She explained.

"Is he in the doghouse"? He asked.

"I wish he was, then I wouldn't be looking for a place". Sydni replied.

"I know the manager of the Sunset Apartments across the street, maybe I can talk to her". Kris offered.

"Thanks anyway Kris, you guys pay me well, but not that good. I can't afford that place". Sydni responded.

"Well let me talk to her first and see what I can come up with.

"Okay, but I only have a little money Kris, don't forget". She said.

The next day, Kris delivered the good news. Mary Beth, of the Sunset apartments had a two-bedroom apartment available and there was a program that offered single mothers luxury apartments for 1/3 of the market price. For $465 a month Sydni could have a two-bedroom, three-bathroom penthouse apartment! "I'll take it! Kris thank you, I could just kiss you". Sydni said.

"I'll take that, or would that fall under sexual harassment"? Kris said laughing.

"Then come over here and give me a hug". Sydni said extending her arms towards him.

Sydni went over on her lunch and signed all the papers. She wrote a check for the security deposit and first months rent. When Mary Beth gave her the keys she felt so relieved. She was feeling extra good when she got home.

Sydni had started packing some of Eric's toys and making plans for renting a U-haul on the weekend. Mike walked in and saw her packing.

"What's going on Sydni"? He asked.

"What! You thought I was playing? Mike, I've barely spoken to you in three weeks. We don't sleep in the same bed. Did you think I was going to live like that forever? I'm out of here. You can have that nasty bitch as your woman. I don't need your ass".

Mike reached over and slapped her. She fell down and reached up and felt her lip. It was bleeding. She knew this was a fight that she wasn't going to win. So she got up and walked out of the room. He was right behind her yelling. "Bitch, I made you. If you think you are gonna leave me and take all my shit, you must be crazy! Take off those earrings and that bracelet. I always said you were ungrateful".

"You know what Mike! You can have this shit because material shit doesn't make me the woman I am. It's your fat ass that needs all the hype to make you the man that you are. If you didn't have the money and clothes, you wouldn't be shit but a fat ass, average ass brotha".

He pulled his hand back to slap her again.

"And if you put your hands on me again, I will be making a call to the Southfield Police to let them know how you make your money and where it is, trust me".

76

Mike put his hand down and said, "bitch don't you take shit I bought out of this house. You leave with what you came with, nothing".

"Gladly Mike, anything to get away from your nasty ass! Oh! And don't you ever believe I'm leaving empty handed, thanks to your dumb ass I have enough to replace all this shit"!

Later that evening Sydni met Blake at "T.G.I.F." and shared her experience.

"Sydni are you sure you want to give it all up because of something so little". Blake asked.

"Little! Blake, his ass fucked someone else and gave me crabs. That's not little to me. If he is doing it like that, he could have given me anything".

"But…you went to the doctor and you are alright. Maybe it was a mistake. You know guys are stupid". Blake said trying to help her friend see both sides.

"Blake, I don't know what you are thinking but just because he's a man, doesn't give him the right to fuck with me and my child's well being. My son needs me. What if he had given me something I couldn't get rid of? Something that could kill me! Then what? I guess some things just matter more to me". Sydni said as she closed her eyes in thought about all the- what if's.-

"I'm sorry Sydni; I just want you to be sure that this is what you want". Blake looked straight into her friend's eyes.

"I'm sure……now let's get drunk and celebrate"! Sydni said.

That weekend, all the girls got together and helped her move. Mike stood guard and made sure she didn't take anything that he had purchased including her jewelry and fur coat. He tried to say that she couldn't take Eric's bedroom set but she just ignored him. As a matter of fact, they all ignored him. She left with all her clothes, Eric's clothes and bedroom set, and a few items that she had purchased with her own money. It didn't seem like much, but her freedom made it seem like a lot.

When the "moving crew" pulled up in front of the apartment building, they were all stunned. "Girl, you are the shit." Mya was astounded at what she saw.

"Wait until you see the apartment, oh! Excuse me, the Penthouse."   Said Rimy who had come down with Sydni several nights before to put up her dishes and groceries.

When they entered the "Penthouse" everyone was geeked. To the right as they walked in, was the laundry room. A little further up also on the right was the guest bathroom, and to the left was a huge kitchen. The living room was big and on one wall there was a doorwall that led to the terrace overlooking the river. The master bedroom was upstairs. It was large and had a full bathroom. Then there was Eric's room which was big and had it's own full bath. His closet was so big they made it into a playroom.

"Hell yeah! Party over here"! Mya said.

"You know it. It's like a whole nother world up here". Sydni exclaimed.

"Does Mike know where you live"? Ariel asked.

"No.....I want him to think that I'm living somewhere off Greenfield. He'll find out soon enough. He thought he was doing something by taking everything back. I still have my self respect- that's more than I can say for him he has none! That's important to me". She stated.

They finally got everything set up and everyone was lying on the floor in the empty living room sipping on wine and beer. It was then that Ariel jumped up and started singing "Count on me through thick and thin, a friendship that will never end. When you are weak I will be strong helping you to carry on. Call on me I will be there, don't be afraid, here's my shoulder you can lean on me. Count on

Me". They all joined in and started singing and waving their hands. Sydni could not have been happier!

Things were going really good for Sydni. Her job was working out swell. She was basically the only office employee besides Marc and Kris. She was handling the books and had started to share in some of the advertising strategies. She was screening prospective employees for the restaurant and assisting the sales team in securing outside accounts. Kris had started to depend on her for everything. Sometimes she felt like she was his wife. Sydni made travel arrangements for him and organized stockholder meetings. She even paid his bills and balanced his checkbook. The trust was there between the two of them.

Sydni's relationship with Marc was a little different, he seemed so stressed all of the time. A few times they had bumped heads, but it was okay. She understood that she couldn't get along with everyone. As long as he didn't disrespect her, he was fine.

Sydni was creating a database for a mass mailing when Ariel called her.

"This is Sydni speaking! What's up girl? Shit, I'm kind of busy. What's up"? Sydni asked.

"I'm going down to Paradise tonight, do you want to go"? Ariel asked.

"Yeah, what time"? Sydni inquired.

"Around nine. Okay"?

Later on that night, as she dressed, she heard her phone rang. She answered it. "Arie I'm on my way."

"On your way where"? Kevin asked.

"Oh! I'm sorry...what's up Kevin"?

"What...you can't call a brother". He asked.

"I'm sorry baby, I've just been busy with work and the bar." Why don't you come out and meet me down at Paradise"? She asked.

"When are you going?" Kevin asked.

"Now, so hurry up. I hear it gets crowded early."

"Bet, I'll see you there". Kevin told her.

When Sydni walked into Paradise, she was pissed she had to pay $10. When she saw Ariel, she stomped over to her".

"You didn't tell me it cost to get in here.....hi Randy". She spoke to Ariel's friend.

"Quit whinning it was only $10. Get yourself a drink".
Said Ariel.

"And I have to buy my own drink"? Sydni asked.

"No you don't have to buy your own drink. What are
you drinking"? Sydni turned around to see who the nice
looking guy was she heard offering her a drink.

"A strawberry daiquiri, please. Thank you, I'm Sydni".

"I'm Trevor".

"It's nice to meet you; sorry you had to hear that. I'm
just mad that they made me pay. Sydni said.

"How much did they charge you"? He asked.

"$10, but I'm straight". Sydni said.

"Here you go". Trevor handed her a ten- dollar bill.

"Let me know if you need anything else". He said as he
went and sat at the bar.

Sydni and Ariel were having a ball their table was filled
with drinks all night. Sydni kept making eye contact with
Trevor. There was something about him that she liked. He
was sitting alone drinking from a bottle of champagne. A
few girls would go over and talk to him from time to time,
but they didn't stay. She also noticed a few guys stopping
by, but he basically kept to himself.

Kevin and his friends came in around eleven. He and his
friends found a table. He bought the two of them more
drinks. Before she realized it, she was super drunk. Kevin
wanted to take her home, but she felt like she could make it

on her own. When she turned back to the bar to tell Trevor good-bye, he was gone.

CHAPTER 6

The next day Sydni's new furniture was delivered. It wasn't as expensive as the furniture Mike had bought her, but it would work. She silently thanked Mike for teaching her a quick lesson in saving her money. Over the prior four months she had managed to save a five-figure dollar amount in her checking account. Later that night Sydni had a date with Kevin. They were suppose to go to the movies, and later get something to eat. Sydni stood in front of her full length mirror checking her looks out. She noticed that she had put on a few pounds. It's funny, she thought, how every guy she met always wanted to go out to eat. She enjoyed the free meals but the pounds were adding up. "I guess I can stand a few pounds." She verbalized, as she turned sideways to get a side view. Her once little butt was beginning to poke out a little. "Go Sydni! Go Sydni"! She said, as she danced around her room putting her hands on her knees and making her booty bounce. She fell on the bed laughing at her self.

That night at Sweetwater Tavern, Kevin asked Sydni a question that she had been trying to avoid.

"So Sydni, when do I get to meet your son"?

"Well Kevin, I don't want to sound negative, but I don't want to introduce another man into my son's life until I know for sure that there is something there".

"So what are you saying about us"? He asked.

"Nothing, quiet as it is kept, I really don't know that much about you. We've been out a few times but I've never asked you if there is someone in your life or questions about your future or anything". She said.

83

"Well, that's because you chose not to. Go ahead and ask me whatever you want". He responded.

"Well, do you have a girlfriend"?

"Not really". He answered.

"Not really? What kind of an answer is that"? Sydni asked.

"Not really, I was with this person for a couple of years and we just have been fading away from each other. I think she is seeing other people now also".

"So you guys were pretty serious then"? Asked Sydni.

"You know how that works". He said.

"O.K. I'm gonna leave that alone, because you keep giving me these vague answers and it's not even necessary. I'm not pressuring you into anything. Which is why I don't think you need to meet my son yet".

"Well whatever". He said.

"I can't believe you have an attitude". Sydni said.

"Sydni I don't have an attitude, it was just a question! So what do you want to go see"?

Sydni finished eating her wings and gave him the I-don't-know shoulder hunch.

Later that evening Kevin offered to walk her up to her apartment. Sydni told him that she was really tired and he didn't have to. She could tell that he was upset but she kissed him and told him that she would call him tomorrow. Once she was settled in she ran a bath and poured a glass of White Zinfandel for herself. As she soaked in the hot water she wondered was she being too hard on Kevin. It wasn't his fault that Mike was such an asshole. "Maybe I should give him a chance. Especially now that I know he doesn't have a girlfriend. I've never been into sharing". She thought.

The wine was starting to give her a slight buzz. She reached for the phone and called his cell phone. His voicemail picked up. "Hi, Kevin, it's Sydni, I just wanted to apologize for tonight. I really like you and I probably was a little harsh. Call me when you get a chance so we can talk. I'll be waiting.

At that very moment Kevin was kissing his girlfriend as she met him at the door of their apartment.

Since Sydni had given up one of her days at the bar. The night that she was there was pretty prosperous. Her regular customers claimed to miss her so they were hooking her up.

Blake was in unusual form. Lately it seemed like she had so much energy. She was down to 165 pounds and you could tell the customers had noticed!"

"Blake, baby you are looking really good". Said Fred a barber who cut hair next door to the bar.

"Thanks, Fred. Did you want another Hennessy and Cranberry"? Blake asked.

"Bring me whatever you want, just come back". Fred said watching her butt as she walked away".

Sydni was humping as usual. When Kevin walked into the bar she waved and blew him a kiss.

"Blake, do me a favor and take these Remys over to Kevin and his friend". Sydni asked.

"So that's Kevin". Said Melanie.

"Yeah, ain't he fine? Replied Sydni.

"Hell yeah! Did you give him some yet"? Melanie asked.

"No, but I think I'm gonna take him home tonight". Sydni stated. "If you don't, I will". Melanie answered with a smile".

The night seemed to fly by. When Sydni walked out of the bar Kevin was waiting for her. His friend was driving so Kevin got into the car with Sydni.

"I can have Jay come get me". Blake replied. "No girl, you don't have to do that! It is enough room, come on! Sydni said. Kevin got in the backseat and let Blake get in.

"I really don't feel good". Blake stated. "What's wrong"? Sydni asked. "I've been having stomach cramps and sometimes I get lightheaded". She replied. "Maybe you should ease up on the pills and that Trimbolic shit. Girl, you look better than ever. You are getting all the play in the bar. Jay is gonna kick your ass if he finds out". Sydni laughed.

"Girl, a diva's work is never done". Blake said as she climbed out and held the seat up for Kevin. "Have fun". She said with a smirk on her face.

"I will, think about what I said. Okay"? Blake stated to Sydni. "Girl, quit worrying about me. I'll be alright"!

On the way to her house, Sydni talked about the bar and what their day had been like. She let herself and Kevin in and Kevin took off his coat. She had a few beers in the fridge and some wine. Sydni gave him a can and poured herself some wine. It had just started to snow and the lights from the passing boats shined into her living room through the terrace window. It was a very calming scene. They watched the boats and just held each other.

Kevin asked where Eric was and Sydni tensed up again. But then she relaxed and told him that he had been spending his weekends over his dad's.

"Let's go upstairs". Sydni took him by the hand and guided him to the stairs. They had barely made it to the top of the stairs before they were tearing each other's clothes off. They fell on the bed and took off what clothing was remaining. Sydni admired his muscular body as she climbed behind him and started to massage his shoulders. She heard his pager go off and stopped rubbing so he could get it. But, he put her hands back around his waist. They resumed kissing but the pager went off again and again. Finally Sydni said. "Do you need to use my phone"?

"No, forget about that. I'm into you right now. Whoever that is can wait". Then his cell phone rang.

"I think whoever that is doesn't want to wait. I have to use the bathroom". Sydni said and got up and went to the bathroom. She heard him answer the phone. It was hard to hear what he was saying because he was whispering, but she heard him say that he would be home shortly and that he was dropping someone off.

"Who was that"? Sydni asked as she came back into the room.

"My boy, something came up with him and I probably won't be able to spend the night".

"You live with your boy"? Sydni asked.

""Huh? No I live by myself. Come here". He started kissing her again.

She knew he was lying but she lay down anyway and Kevin got on top of her. Sydni realized that he hadn't pulled out a condom, so she reached over into her nightstand and pulled one out.

"Oh yeah"! He said. As he pulled up on his knees to put it on she noticed on his arm. She sat up and saw that it was a tattoo.

"What does that say"? She asked.

"Nothing". He said as he pushed her back down.

"What does it say Kevin"? Sydni asked again.

"It says Juanita"? -----------"Who the hell is Juanita"? Sydni asked as she pushed him off her.

"Sydni come on now. This tattoo is old as hell. Come on baby, I'm horny as hell". He said.

"Is Juanita your girlfriend that you are fading away from"? Sydni asked.

"Do we really have to discuss this now? The only person I'm thinking about is you. Now come here and let me kiss those pouty lips". Against her better judgment Sydni succumbed to temptation.

After they finished making love, Kevin drifted off to sleep. His pager was still going off, so Sydni picked it up and tiptoed into the bathroom. It was overloaded with pages, all to the same number. Sometimes followed by 911. So, Sydni called the number. She knew she was wrong, but she felt like she had to do it.

A woman picked up on the first ring. "Where are you, damnit"? "Excuse me"? Sydni responded.

"Who is this"? The woman asked. -----"This is Sydni, who are you"? "I must have paged the wrong number, I'm looking for Kevin". She exclaimed.

"No, you paged the right number. Who is this"? Sydni asked.

"This is his woman, Juanita. Where the fuck is he"? She asked. ---- "His woman? He told me he didn't have a woman. You know I hate to be the one to tell you, but we both have been getting played. That bastard is laying in my bed sleep". Sydni confided.

Juanita began to cry. She explained to Sydni that they had been together for four years and this wasn't the first time he had done this to her. Sydni assured her that she really didn't know about her and that she was through with him. She told her that she should be too. She knew from the sound of her voice that Juanita would forgive him.

"I'll let you speak to this sorry motherfucker. Because he is about to get the fuck out of my house"! Sydni walked into her room and Kevin was still snoring.

"Get up asshole. The phone is for you". Sydni said as she stood over him.

Kevin woke up and wiped the slob from the side of his mouth. "What"? He asked. –"Get the damn phone". Exclaimed Sydni.

Kevin picked up the phone he tried to explain but Sydni stopped him. "Really Kevin you don't have to explain. I just know that you are the typical no-good ass brotha on a pussyhunt. I'm fine the person I feel sorry for is your girl! Now if you would get your sorry ass up out of my bed, I'd like to go to sleep".

"Sydni....it doesn't even have to be like this". Kevin pleaded. --- "Correction asshole. It didn't have to be like this. You could have told the truth in the first place. Just get out". She said pointing to the door.

Kevin gathered his things and Sydni walked him to the door. --- And, I don't appreciate you slobbing on my pillow." Sydni gave him a final verbal jab as she slammed the door behind him. She slid down to the floor and put her head in her hands. Oh well, at least I relieved some of my sexual frustration. I'm starting to think that's all these brothas are good for. She got up when she heard the phone ringing. "What now"? She thought. It was Kevin.

"I forgot I didn't drive. Can you take me home"? He asked. – "You have got to be joking. Kevin if you were White you would definitely be blonde". She hung up the phone.

The next day at Mama's Sydni went over the whole evening with everyone. They all thought it was funny.

"We aren't through with that brotha. Guys get off too easy. He probably went home to that crying ass girl and sucked up to her and now everything is alright." Mya exclaimed.

"I really don't care Mya, it's not like I was in love with him. He basically was a free meal and a little change here and there. So at worst I have to pay my own phone bill"!

Ariel laughed "you are funny as hell Sydni. " Where is Blake"? Sydni asked.

"She said she would be over later because she wasn't feeling good". Ariel answered.

"What's up with her lately"? Mya asked. "It's like she is obsessed with losing weight. She has already lost enough. She won't be cute if she gets too little". Ariel commented.

"Mama, I think you should say something to her. I've mentioned it a couple times and she just keeps ignoring me." Sydni replied. At that moment Blake walked through the door. She didn't seem like she was sick though, actually she was upbeat.

"I thought you were sick." Mama asked. – "No, I'm straight I just needed to take some trimbolic and go to the gym". She said.

"Listen Blake, we are all worried about you taking so many of those damn diet pills and drinking that shit. Your doctor couldn't have prescribed so much shit"! Mama's voice had a serious tone in it.

"I thought y'all wanted me to lose weight. What? Y'all liked me better when I was fat and miserable"? She screamed.

"Whoa, we are just concerned. Nobody wants you to be unhappy. But, we don't want you to kill yourself either! One minute you are doing cartwheels then the next minute you're dazed and disoriented and nauseated. Blake, something isn't right about what you are doing." Sydni pleaded to her friend.

"It must be right because I'm losing weight and I feel good about myself again". Blake tossed her purse on the table and a pill case fell out.

"Fuck that, I'm not going to sit around and watch you overdose on this shit." Said Mya as she grabbed the case and made her way to the sink. Blake pushed a chair over and tried to get to Mya, but Ariel and Sydni grabbed her before she could get to Mya.

"No Mya.......please don't do that! I need them. Please don't." Blake screamed and tried to get away from her two friends but they wouldn't let her go. Mya poured the pills down the drain and ground them up in the disposal. Blake fell to the floor and cried.

"I can't believe you let them do this to me Mama". She cried. –"Blake, it's for the best. Look at you. You are no better than Jay right now. Can't you see you are addicted? What about your kids?" Suddenly Blake began to breathe hard, her heart seemed like it was going to burst from her chest. She put her hand on her chest and tried to catch her breath.

"Blake, what's wrong"? Mama asked as she walked towards her. "I can't breathe! Mama help me"! Blake gasped for breath.

"Someone call 911"! Mama screamed. Blake collapsed to the floor.

Mya rode with Blake to the hospital. She watched as the Paramedics worked on her in the Ambulance. They were saying a lot of medical lingo that she didn't quite understand. So, she decided to pray. "Lord, I know that I don't really pray very often. And Lord knows when was the last time I've been to church. But I need a huge favor and I will start going on a regular basis. Lord, please help Blake. I feel so guilty. I know I shouldn't have taken the pills from her but I don't want her to hurt herself. Now look at her. Lord, I just need you to make sure that she is okay. She has babies to take care of. And she is the only one that cooks for me when I need her to. Our crew will never for give me if something happens to her. Please Lord let her make it. We need her, amen." A single tear fell from her eye and landed on her hand that held Blake's hand.

Once Blake was admitted, Ariel went to call Jay. Everyone else sat and waited in the waiting room. No one felt like talking. It seemed like everyone was locked in his or her own personal prayer. When Jay arrived he looked bad. It was obvious that his habit was getting worse. His clothes were wrinkled and he hadn't shaved in days. He looked a mess. Mama filled him in on what the doctors had said, which really wasn't much. She was still being seen and there had been no word on her condition. Sydni said, "I feel so bad, I knew she wasn't feeling good and I didn't do anything about it. Remember she was stumbling at the bar"?

"Sydni you can't feel bad about this. How were we supposed to know it had gotten this bad"? Ariel commented to Sydni.

"Because we are friends, her sisters. You pick up on things like that. That's what I'm saying, I saw her getting worse and I didn't stop her". Sydni lamented.

"You cannot believe that this is your fault"! Mama said. – "No Mama, it's all of our faults". Sydni said as she walked out of the room.

"Don't worry Mama, she'll be alright. She is just upset right now". Ariel said to Mama.

Mya elbowed Jay in the ribs he was nodding off. "You need to be getting some help yourself, don't you"? She asked Jay.

"I'm straight, I'm just tired". He said. Mya just looked at him.

At that point the doctor walked in. He explained that in essence Blake had poisoned her self by taking a mixture of pills. This in turn caused her heart rate to rise to dangerous levels. She had received a blood transfusion and was in the intensive care unit. The doctor said that we could each go in one at a time to see her. Jay went in first for a few minutes. He came out and told Mama he was going to call the kids and let them know that their mom was all right. Mama and Ariel each went in after Jay and then Sydni.

Blake looked terrible it almost made Sydni sick. She looked smaller than ever in that big white bed. All the tubes and wires made things seem grave to Sydni. When she got to the side of the bed, she took Blake's hand in hers and kissed it putting it to her face. She said a small prayer and was getting ready to leave when Blake slowly opened her eyes. She didn't have the strength to say anything, but somehow Sydni knew that she was saying that everything was gonna be all right. She bent down and gave Blake a kiss and walked out of the room.

Walking back to the waiting room Sydni's heart felt a little lighter after seeing her friend open her eyes. Somehow, someway, she knew that Blake would be okay. By the time that she reached the room they had decided what "shifts" each would take until Blake was released. Mama and Jay took the first shift, so the girls left and went back to Mama's. When they got there the next hour was spent filling Paige and Rimy in on the details. Rimy agreed to watch Blake's kids until Jay got back. It was gonna be a long day.

Over night there was no bad news received about Blake. She was still progressing. Sydni was dropping Eric off at the day care center when her cell phone rang.

"Hello....What's up Sydni"? --"Who's speaking?" She asked.

"Damn, you don't even recognize my voice anymore." Said Syrus. – "Sy? What do you want"? Sydni asked.

"Are you still mad at me"? He asked.

"It's not about me being mad. I just don't want to deal with you anymore Sy! We've already talked about this". Sydni replied.

"Didn't I tell you that brotha wouldn't last? I heard through the grapevine that you moved out".

Damn, who told his ass, she thought to herself.

"I also heard that you copped a place in the Sunset Apartments and I know you need help with that rent, it ain't no joke. Why don't you let a brotha back in, so I can help you out a little"?

Sydni thought about it for a minute, it would be nice to be back in his pocket. "Sy...go to hell and lose my number." She hung up the phone and smiled to herself.

"First time shame on you. Second time shame on me".

After getting settled at work Sydni dropped Blake a line. The doctor's wanted to keep her for another day of observation. She was feeling a lot better. Sydni told her about Syrus and she laughed.

"Girl, what did you do to him"? Blake asked.

"Nothing, he is just now seeing that he had a good thing. You know, they never miss it until it's gone. I know one thing I miss about him, all ten of those inches. Brotha had it going on in that department. It took me three times before I could master that, but I worked it out. Besides it gets lonely on the road. Those groupies can't offer him what I was giving him". Sydni said.

"Has Mike been calling"? Blake asked.

"Every now and then. I think he is getting the picture". Sydni told Blake about Kevin and his girlfriend.

"I knew he was too good to be true, with his fine ass". Said Blake. She winced as she reached over to her nightstand to get her water. "I'm ready to go home and eat some real food".

"Oh! Now you ready to eat. You have to damn near have a heart attack before you realize that you need food, huh". Laughed Sydni.

"Ya'll don't have to worry about that shit anymore. I'm through with the diets. I probably will still exercise though when I get the O.K. I like my weight right now and I like myself. Sydni I want to thank you for trying to be a real friend even when I wouldn't let you. I should have been listening to you all the time, but I got caught up". Blake exclaimed.

"You know Blake we all get caught up one time or another and we have to make our own mistakes. But the next time you scare the hell out of me like this, I'm gonna kill you myself. Now get some rest I'll pick you up tomorrow". Sydni hung the phone up and thanked God for saving her friend.

Later on that day Marc came into the office. When Sydni spoke to him, he walked right past her. He must be in one of those moods, she thought. Eric's teacher had called her earlier and told her that Eric was running a fever. She did some billing and organized the personnel files while she waited for her to call back. She went into Marc's office and asked him if there was anything special that he needed her to do because she might be leaving early because of her baby. Marc waved her off and continued to talk on the phone.

Eric's teacher did call back and state that he still wasn't feeling well and that she should come and get him. As she was gathering her things to leave, Marc came and set a memo that he needed typed on her desk.

"Marc, I have to go pick up Eric from school. He isn't feeling well".

"Sydni, that is not my problem. We pay you to be here, and I need this typed and distributed before you leave"! Marc said as he slammed his office door.

Sydni stood there for a minute contemplating whether or not to curse him out or save face and type the memo. She settled for the latter. It took her twenty minutes to complete the task. Sydni was steaming. "I told his ass I had to leave and he brought this last minute shit up here". She thought as she gathered her things and left without saying goodbye.

When Sydni picked Eric up from the daycare he was still feeling warm and had started vomiting. She decided to take him to urgent care. She called his dad and told him where they would be in case he wanted to come there. She always made sure she kept him involved in situations like this. It seemed only fair since Eric lived with her. Big Eric had to admit that she was one of the better "baby mommas" out there. She never harassed him for money because she felt she shouldn't have to make someone take care of his or her own child. Sydni wasn't concerned about who he was dating because what they had was over. She trusted his judgment and knew that he wouldn't have her child around someone that would harm him in any way.

As she pulled up to Urgent Care, Big Eric was already there. He immediately came and picked Little E up out of the car and carried him in. Sydni smiled and thought to herself. It was amazing how much they looked alike. Little E had that same Indian red complexion that his dad had. Once he was signed in they all sat in the waiting room.

"I'm about sick of emergency rooms and hospitals. I've had two friends in the hospital in the last 6 months." Sydni explained to Big Eric what had been going on.

"How have you been holding up"? He asked. "What do you mean"? Sydni asked

"I mean, how are you doing since you moved. You know I don't get in your business, but I just wondered if you were doing okay". He said.

"Eric you know I'm gonna be all right. If I managed to get over you, this will be a synch." She joked. Eric and Sydni had been everybody's dream couple. They were like best friends. It's just that Sydni kept growing and Eric stopped. He was in and out of work and she would work two jobs at a time. She finally got tired of the instability and broke it off. They had a few relapses every now and then, but she would never let it get serious again. She would always love him, but she didn't think she could be in love with him again.

After the doctor saw Little Eric, he gave him a prescription for an antibiotic. Big Eric followed them to the apartment. He sat with Little E until he went to sleep. Sydni offered him a beer and they sat down in the living room to talk. Their conversation was about their current adventures in the dating game. Sydni pointed out that she was through with the game for a minute. Eric stated to her that he dated a lot but was never serious about any of the women.

"I haven't been in a serious relationship since you Sydni." He said.

"I wish I could say the same." Sydni replied. "It's like when I start to date someone they always want to claim me right away".

"And they should Sydni. You are a good girl! I don't blame them one bit, I swear.....you don't miss the water until the wells gone dry. Sometimes I wish we were still together". He said.

"You know Eric, you never know what the future holds". Said Sydni.

"Yeah right! That's what you always say to keep me at bay." He said. They laughed and once Eric finished his beer, he went upstairs and kissed his son. As he was leaving, he turned and said: "Are you sure you don't want some company later on"? He questioned.

"No thank you Eric, but when I do, I'll keep you in mind".

He bent down and kissed her on the forehead. "Take care of yourself and him. Call me if he needs anything else....or you".

She interrupted him. "Goodbye silly". And closed the door.

CHAPTER 7

Sydni spent the rest of the day in bed with Eric watching Sesame Street & Disney movies. It was really refreshing. Later that night her phone rang, it was Mya.

"Hey girl, I just wanted to tell you our mission is complete".

"What mission"? Sydni asked.

"That brotha Kevin will be sorry he ever messed with you." - "Oh goodness! Mya what did you do"? She asked.

"I put Vaseline all over all of his car windows and put dog shit under his door handles".

"Mya that is gross! You are crazy girl! I'll talk to you tomorrow".

The next day at work, Kris informed Sydni that he needed her to plan a trip for him, a friend, and his children to Hawaii. She discussed what had happened the day before with Marc. He told her not to worry about it. Sydni felt comfortable with Kris, he was just so cool.

That afternoon Marc came in and was acting totally different. He acted like nothing had happened. He came in and spoke to her asking her to schedule a meeting with all 12 shareholders for the next week. This included a luncheon. She made reservations at the Roostertail and booked the conference room for the time he needed. His change of behavior surprised her, but she thought, oh well.

At one o'clock a woman came into the office to meet Marc for an interview. Sydni was surprised to hear that because she had been doing the interviews for the restaurant. She showed her to his office.

Sydni had just finished a mass mailing of announcement cards when the woman came out of Marc's office. He introduced her as Lillian the new Controller. Sydni shook her hand and welcomed her aboard. Marc explained that Lillian would be taking over all of the accounts payable and receivable duties that she had been taking care of. In a way this was a relief and would lighten her workload. But for some reason Sydni felt like this was just the beginning.

It was Thursday, Ariel, Sydni, and Mya went to the Paradise. They found a table and were waiting for a waitress when Sydni spotted Trevor. He was standing over by the DJ booth. He looked so cute in some gray jogging pants and a black, gray and red Nike T-shirt. He also had on brand new Airmax with those same colors in them. He was standing with a group of guys. Sydni knew one of the guys from her high school. Moments later she walked over and spoke to Jalil, then to Trevor. After kicking it with Jalil for a minute, Trevor asked her what she was drinking.

After getting her drink, she asked Trevor what he had been up to. He said: "Thinking about you".

"Really"? Don't start using the typical lines on me now." She said.

"I have". Said Trevor. "Last week I had to leave and you were gone when I got back. Do you think we could exchange numbers this time, he asked?" "Sure". She answered.

They exchanged numbers and Sydni went back over to her table. Ariel and Mya were getting their drink on and dancing at the table. A fine ass chocolate brother came up and asked Sydni to dance. She accepted the invitation and went on to the dance floor. Just as they reached the floor the DJ switched to a slow song so the guy grabbed her by the waist. As they started to dance she looked over at Trevor and their eyes locked. He didn't look happy and it made her feel uncomfortable. She almost felt like she was cheating. After the song was over she excused her self and walked off the dance floor. When she reached her table Ariel told her that Trevor had sent her another drink. She looked over to where he was standing to thank him for the drink but he was gone! She watched the door all night long to see if he was going to return, but he never came back. Driving home Sydni was thinking. "What the hell are you tripping for girl, he is not your man. You don't know anything about him. Then why do I feel guilty she asked herself"?

Sydni couldn't stop thinking about Trevor. There was something cool and mysterious about him. She was mystified at him sending her another drink and then just disappearing for the night. He definitely had her attention as evidenced by her watching the door for the rest of the night waiting and sub-consciously hoping that he would return. There was something about this brotha that was different.

A few weeks had passed when Shawntel called Sydni and asked her to meet her at Fishbones Rhythm Kitchen in Southfield for a drink. It had been three months since they had gotten together. Mama was able to keep Eric, so they got dressed and dropped him off with her. When she got there Shawntel was already seated and waved her over.

"What's up girl friend? You're looking good as usual". Shawntel said.

"Girl this is just a little something I put together". Sydni had on a pair of black slacks by Dkny and a red wrap around blouse that tied at the back. She had a black fitted leather jacket with some black Gucci loafers and a red Coach backpack.

"I see you've put on a little weight too". Shawntel cracked.

"Yeah, in all the right places". Sydni said as she slapped her butt.

They ordered drinks and an appetizer. The two were busy laughing and talking when Sydni caught a glimpse of someone approaching out of the corner of her eye. She never moved her head waiting for the person to come into full view. It was Trevor! She wondered what had brought him there. Trevor was looking superb in cream gabardine slacks with a cream mock shirt and a cream and red houndstooth sport coat. He topped it off with some spit shined red gators.

Sydni was surprised and glad to see him because she hadn't been down to the Paradise in a couple of weeks and she had paged him once but he didn't call back, so she never called again.

"Well, well, what's up lady? Can I get a hug"? He asked.

"Nothing at all, how are you? She asked. –It's my birthday, so me and my boys are hanging out". He said.

"Oh a boys night out, huh"?

"Yeah, but maybe you can give me a call tomorrow and we can go out". Said Trevor.

104

"I think I called you once before and you don't return your pages so, I'll leave it up to you to give me a call". Sydni boldly stated. They exchanged numbers again and he went back and sat down with his friends. Sydni asked their waitress to send him a drink and tell him she said happy birthday. She and Shawntel finished their drinks and headed out the door. She waved as they left.

"Okay, what's the story with him"? Shawntel asked.

"Nothing really, I met him at the Paradise a few weeks ago but I've only called him once and he didn't return the page so I filed his number away. I really don't know much about him".

The next day came and went still no call from Trevor. Sydni hadn't noticed until later on that day when she reached in her pocket and felt something. When she saw it was his number, she almost called but changed her mind. I have never chased a man down; I'm not about to start now.

The weather was finally getting better. It was a warm day so Sydni decided to rock her new chocolate Michael Kors suit that she had bought from Saks to work. She put a carmel colored blazer over it so that she would still be dressed for work. Kris had agreed to meet Sydni for lunch to discuss some of the marketing strategies that she had come up with. She also planned to discuss the new addition to the office staff. Sydni had found Lillian to be exactly what her title was. She was the new Controller and she wanted to control everything. The relationship that Sydni had developed with their vendors had rapidly been destroyed. Lillian had her own "new and improved" way of paying the bills. But, Sydni had complete confidence that Kris would help her fix the problem.

When Sydni arrived back at her office, Lillian was over at her desk going through some of her files.

"Excuse me Lillian, is there something I can get for you"? Sydni asked. Lillian noticed the agitation in Sydni's voice immediately.

"I'm sorry Sydni, I just thought it would be okay for me to move the personnel files over near my desk, since I am taking over payroll. I mean that is part of my job as the Controller".

"Lillian, I wouldn't have had a problem moving the files over there. But I do have a problem with you rambling through my desk. In the future I'd appreciate it if you would wait until I get here".

"Well Sydni, our business day starts at 8:30 not 9:00, so I assumed you were taking some more time off".

"Let's get one thing straight now, you are not my boss. You do not assign my hours. My personal time off is none of your business. In case you didn't know I am salaried not hourly and I get my work done plus some, in the time I am here. So, I would advise you to check the chain of command and find some other underdog to try to control. And I'm through talking about it. With that Sydni went to the closet to hang up her blazer. Lillian's face had turned beet red and she looked like she wanted to say something else but thought better of it and went back to her desk.

You could have cut the tension with a knife in the office. Kris came in displaying his usual happy self, but neither Sydni nor Lillian spoke when he said, "hello". "Sydni what's up? Why is everyone so quiet"? There was still no answer. Then Sydni asked him. "Are we still doing lunch"?

He responded. "Yeah, are you ready"? Sydni said that she was. She got up, got her blazer and stomped down the stairs.

Sydni had made reservations at Sinbad's on the river. Once they were seated she started to tell him everything that had been happening over the past two weeks, including her argument with Lillian, and the incident with Marc. When she finally finished Kris handed her a glass of water and waited for her to catch her breath.

"Sydni, if you have a problem with the way someone is treating you in the office, I need you to come to me immediately. Don't wait two weeks later. We can nip these situations in the bud, right away. I guess Lillian is going to network all of our billing and payroll into one system. Maybe Marc should have told you before he made that decision, but I thought he had already discussed it with you or I would have. I probably should let you know that he has informed me that he is also interviewing for a Marketing Manager". Sydni's mouth dropped to the floor.

"Kris you are taking the Marketing from me too". She asked.

"It's not my decision. The shareholders feel that we need someone who majored in Marketing to head the Marketing Division".

"In other words someone with a degree". She said.

"I guess you could say that. But, don't worry Sydni, your job is secure". Kris said.

"As what, a Clerk, Administrative Assistant? Kris you know my skills span wider than that. The Shareholders didn't have a problem with my marketing when I helped secure our first three hundred accounts, now did they"?

"I know Sydni, but it's out of my hands". Said Kris.

"This is some bullshit... you know that"? Sydni responded.

Don't worry we'll work it out, I promise". Kris said.

Sydni didn't get everything out of the meeting with Kris that she wanted. It was clear that he had a lot of good intentions, but in reality his hands were tied with respect to what was happening to her. When they got back to the office from lunch, Sydni had to run across the street to her home and get a change of clothes for Eric. As she was returning to the office she noticed a gentleman getting out of his Range Rover. As she passed by she politely spoke and kept walking. The man called to her.

"Excuse me do you have a minute"?

"Actually I don't. I'm already late getting back". She said.

"Can I at least get a name"? He asked.

"My name is Sydni and yours"? - I am Larue and it's a pleasure to meet you".

"Larue huh? The pleasure is all mine". She said.

"Hopefully, I can kidnap you one day and take you to lunch".

"I don't think you would have to kidnap me, I think I would come willingly". She said.

"Well, then it's a date". When can I call you"? Larue asked.

"You can call me at this number". She said handing him a card. "Talk to you soon".

When she got upstairs she looked out of the window and saw him go across the street to her complex. He used a key to get in the gate! She couldn't believe he stayed in the same complex as hers and she hadn't seen him before. He was pretty good looking. He had to be about 6'2", 240 lbs. He dressed very nice. He had on a black suit with a sweet colorful tie, with some black gators. She also noticed he was bowlegged. Not bad she thought. It was back to business as her extension rang.

"This is Sydni." - "I was just checking to make sure this wasn't a bogus number you gave me". Larue stated.

"Now do you think I would do something like that"? She asked.

"The way you were so intent on walking past me....I don't know". He said.

"Trust me if I didn't want you to have the number I wouldn't have given it to you". She said.

"How about lunch tomorrow?" He asked. – "You move pretty fast, don't you think"? She asked.

"Only when I see something I want." He replied. – "Really? Then tomorrow it is. Let's say around one"? Sydni stated.

"Bye." She said as she hung up the phone smiling. "Maybe this isn't such a bad day after all". She thought.

The following day they met for lunch at the Mesquite Grill. Larue was looking good as hell in a navy blue suit. His tie had navy blue, light blue and white in it. He had a fresh haircut and smelled good. Sydni made it a point to wear something that showed off her newfound curves. She picked out a peach pants suit. The jacket was fitted and the pants were stretched material. She had some cream Nine-West heels and a matching purse.

They made a stunning couple and everyone watched them walk to their table. Larue knew a lot of people there and stopped and talked to a few guys that he had gone to school with. He made sure to introduce Sydni that made her feel special. One of his buddies told her she was very pretty. She accepted this compliment gracefully and thanked him. During lunch she found out that he owned his own business operating in downtown Detroit. It was an Office Delivery Business. He shared the fact that he had been living in the Sunset Apartments for five years. Time seemed to fly by them. Their conversation flowed continuously with ease. Sydni almost didn't notice that most of the lunch crowd had finished and left. She told him that they probably should wrap it up. He dropped her back off at work after he made her promise that they would do this again.

When Sydni returned to her office Marc was waiting to talk to her. He asked her to come to his office. She went in and sat down. He started out by stating that her lunch period would have to start being that, just one hour. He also told her that he didn't appreciate her going to Kris about him. Sydni told him that it was her understanding that there was an open door policy and she felt comfortable enough to talk to Kris. She said that she did not feel the same about him. She also said that since they were on the subject, she didn't appreciate him not discussing with her the new moves being made in the office, especially since they affected her directly. They squared off for a few minutes and then Sydni stormed out of his office and slammed the door. She went to the restroom to calm down and wash her face off. "What the hell am I going to do now?" She thought.

Sydni had a lot on her mind, mostly about her working conditions and the many changes that she was being put through. Her relationship with Marc had deteriorated to its lowest point. So, when Mya called and suggested that the girls get together, she was all for it.

It was the first time that all of the girls had gotten together since Blake's incident. They were all looking good and smelling good as they stepped into the Paradise. Sydni was ready for anything. She was pumped up from the shots of Tequila that they drank at her apartment. The club was packed. Once they found a table, the drinks started flowing. Sydni and Mya were locked in a boring conversation with a set of twins. Blake and Ariel were cracking up. Finally a hustle song came on and that was their break. They all went to the floor and were having a good time doing their thing when a fight broke out. The Bouncers stepped right in and stopped it. They put the fighters out.

Sydni saw Trevor back in the poolroom when she walked in, but she didn't stop and speak. She observed him making his way around to her. He stopped in front of her but didn't say anything. She stared him down and walked away. As she went to the restroom she had to squeeze past a group of guys, one who just happened to be Mike.

"What's up girl"? Mike asked. - "How are you"? Sydni asked.

"I'm fine. You're looking good as usual". He said.

"So are you Mike...fuck any skanky hoes lately"? She said as she walked away from him.

When she got to the restroom it was filled with ghetto girls smoking weed and cigarettes. She heard one of the girls say. "Did you see Trevor's ass out there? He thinks he is the shit don't he?" Her girlfriend nodded her head in agreement. Sydni looked past them and slid into a stall. When she was finished she squeezed between two girls at the sink to wash her hands.

Ariel was coming in the door as Sydni was leaving. "Just checking on your drunk ass. You were gone for a long time". She said.

"I'm straight, it is just jam packed in there." She said. After that she saw that same chocolate brother she had danced with before and asked him for another dance. When she got out on the floor she saw Trevor getting freaked down by some Hoochie mama. She was salty at first but then she started to do her own booty dancing with sexy chocolate. She caught Trevor watching her through the wall mirror, he wasn't looking happy. Sydni loved it. She saw Mike glaring at her and she danced even harder. Tonight was her night to shine. She had all her girls with her and they were all getting blew back!

When Sydni got back to her table there was a bottle of champagne sitting in an ice bucket. She asked the waitress who it was from? She pointed to Mike. Sydni shook her head and sent it back. Then she ordered her own bottle then popped the cork and poured each of her girls a glass. She gave a toast to getting over no good ass brothas. She was drunk by the end of the night and didn't notice Trevor walking up to her.

"Where are you going without saying bye"? He asked.

"I'm going home, why"? Said a drunken Sydni.

"Can I go"? Trevor asked. - "I don't think so. What happen to that Hoochie mama you were dancing with? I'm sure she wouldn't mind taking you home with her". Sydni replied.

"Why are you tripping? You definitely weren't by yourself all night. And who was that brotha that bought you that bottle of Moet"? He asked with a slight attitude.

"Did I miss something here? When did y'all get together?" Ariel asked.

"You are right Ariel". "Trevor you are free to dance with whoever you want. You are not my man. Shit, I can't even get you to call back my pages".

"I don't know why you are acting like this but I'll call you tomorrow." Trevor said. - "Whatever". Said Sydni.

"What was that all about girl"? Ariel asked.

"I don't know. I haven't seen or heard from him in weeks then I saw him the other day at Fishbones. It's something about him Ariel; I just can't put my finger on it". Sydni exclaimed.

"I know he must have some cheddar because I saw him pull out a bankroll a few times and he just pulled off in a new caddy". Blake replied.

"You know that's the last thing I'm worried about Blake. I can handle my own." Sydni said.

"Ain't nothing like a little help". Blake added.

"I heard that". Mya added her two cents.

Blake drove Sydni home she kept saying that she was sleepy. Sydni called in sick the next day.

Sydni's whole day was spent nursing a hangover. Paige had called and asked if she would take her to look at some prom dresses. Sydni tried to drag herself out of bed. Eric was running all over the house and she knew it wouldn't be long before something was broken. When she finally got up her head started spinning and she headed straight for the bathroom. Eric followed her in and watched as she threw up.

"Mama have you been drinking drugs"? He asked.

She almost choked from laughing as she vomited. "No baby, momma hasn't been drinking drugs". She said.

"Should I call 9-1-1?" He asked. —"No honey, I'll be alright." At least he knows who to call she thought.

Sydni began to feel better. After she showered she threw on a pink and white K-Swiss jogging suit and some white classics. She dressed Eric and then went to pick up Paige. She had been doing a lot better since the abortion. Sydni could hardly believe that she was graduating already.

Sydni took Paige out to Birmingham and looked in some of the dress shops out there. She assured her that she didn't have to pick anything that day. Sydni agreed to buy her shoes and accessories. They stopped at Max and Erma's on old Woodward. Paige was really excited about the prom. She and Zo had been getting along well and she couldn't wait to show him off in a tuxedo to her friends.

114

"So Paige, what college have you been accepted at". Sydni asked.

Paige hesitated and answered. "None". – Sydni looking surprised replied. "What do you mean none"?

"I'm not ready to jump back into school yet Sydni. I need a break. I want to take some time off and figure out what direction I want to go".

"Well okay, but you know you need to have your ass in school. At least somewhere locally". Sydni said.

Sydni could hear Mama screaming already. She was gonna be pissed off. It was bad enough that Sydni was still going to school part-time when time permitted. She had been so busy with the bar and the brewery that she had sat out the winter and spring semesters. Sydni still wasn't feeling a 100%, so they decided to call it a day after they ate. Paige went back to Sydni's place to work on the computer and watch Eric while Sydni took a nap.

Sydni was awaken when she felt someone nudging her. It was Eric with the cordless phone in his hand.

"Momma the phone is for you". He said. – "Thank you E". She said.

"Hello" Sydni answered. – "What's up girl"? The voice answered. – "Who's speaking"? Sydni asked.

"It's Trevor". Her heart skipped a beat.

"Really? What's up with you playboy"? She asked.

"Naw, it seems like you got the best hand". Trevor stated.

"This is a surprise". Said Sydni. – "Why is that"? He asked.

"I noticed last night that you seem to be the man up in that joint. I didn't figure you would have time for little old me, with all those hoodrats chasing you". Trevor laughed.

"I don't have anybody chasing me. I'm chasing you. What's up for tonight"? He asked.

Sydni remembered that she had promised Larue that they could go to the show. "Well, I already have plans for tonight, maybe we can go out tomorrow". She stated.

"Yeah, well give me a call. You have the number". He then hung up the phone. "I know that was not an attitude that I heard in his voice. And the Negro didn't even let me say bye. He is so rude". " Then why do I like him she thought"?

That night Larue met her out front and they went to a movie theater in Grosse Pointe Woods. Their conversation bordered on the professional level. Every now and then they would stick in personal points. Larue revealed to his reasoning behind his opening the type of business he had. In college he had a promising career in football until one day he was in an automobile accident on his way to class. It took a long time for him to heal and he was never the same. He stated. So after he finished college with a Business Management Degree, he decided that he wanted to help people that were in the same position that he had been in.

Sydni was almost crying by the time that he finished his story. "I'm really impressed Larue". She said.

They finally arrived at the theater and picked a movie. They had just enough time to get their snacks and find a seat in the back. The lights dimmed as they were sitting down. Larue put his arms around the back of her chair. She noticed and leaned into his armpit. The first preview had not gone off the screen before Larue started rubbing her thigh. This made her a little uncomfortable. She moved his hand off of her thigh and then he started kissing her neck. Sydni straightened up in the seat and told him to slow down a little. He laughed and watched the next preview. Before that one was over he was kissing her neck again and he grabbed her hand and put it on his penis. Before she could snatch her hand away, he stuck his tongue in her ear. Why did he do that? She wondered as she became agitated.

Sydni had reached her boiling point. She snatched her hand away and sat up in her seat responding.

"Look you are making me really uncomfortable. I think I'm ready to go home".

"Damn calm down. I'm just trying to relax you a little". Larue said.

"Well, that ain't the way. I know you don't think because you spent $20 damn dollars at the show that you are suppose to get a piece of ass. I don't know you like that yet". Sydni replied in a not so nice tone.

"Well you didn't have a problem getting in my damn truck and riding all the way out here with a stranger". He said.

By now the entire row of people in front and in back of them were listening.

"You know what.....you are right. So how about this? Your horny ass don't have to worry about me riding back with you". Sydni said as she got up and excused herself down the aisle.

When she got out of the theater she whipped her cell phone out and tried the house. Paige must have been asleep because she wasn't answering the phone. She called Mya and Ariel but she got no response. Blake was at home, but didn't have a car at her disposal. By now Sydni was near tears. She was beginning to regret her outburst because she couldn't find a way home. He was wrong as two left shoes and she knew that for sure.

Finally, Larue came outside and tapped her on her shoulder.

"Sydni, I'm sorry. I behaved like an animal and I hope you will accept my apology. I don't know what got into me. I cannot lie and say that I'm not physically attracted to you because I am. I'm used to dealing with females that have their eyes on the prize so they are with that".

"Well Larue, I'm not like that and I'm very disappointed that this is the way you perceived me".

"If it's not to late I'd like to make it up to you. Can I start by taking you to this Ice Cream Parlor down the street"? He said.

Even though Sydni was still mad, and had her mind made up that she would never speak to him again after that night, she reluctantly agreed to go.

They stopped at Ben and Jerry's Ice Cream Parlor and each got a cone. There were a couple of uncomfortable moments of silence a few times but they made it through the rest of the evening. When he pulled up in front of the apartment, she breathed a sigh of relief.

Sydni was mentally exhausted and just wanted to go to bed alone. Larue knew not to even think about asking to come up to her place. She thanked him for a good time and got out of the truck. She made it a point not to ask him to call her the next day. When she got upstairs Eric was asleep in her bed. So much for sleeping alone, she thought. She moved his little body over and fell into a coma.

Sydni was starting to hate going to work and it was hard as hell for her to wake up the next morning. She took an extra long shower and woke Paige and Eric up. They all ate a bowl of cereal. Sydni raced to get them to school on time. She loved having her sisters over because they were a huge help with Eric. Plus, they were at the age where they were a lot of fun.

It was back to work for Sydni. She was relieved when she saw that no one else had gotten there yet. She started her work and her day was going well until the phone range. It was Larue!

"Hey Sydni, I just wanted to call and apologize again for last night. I was wondering would you like to go to lunch"?

"Thanks, but no thanks Larue, I'm really busy today. I'm the only one here and the phones have been ringing like crazy. I have to go troubleshoot a problem in the restaurant". She said.

"Well, give me a call when you're free". He said.

Sydni wanted to say, "I'll never be free, ever again psycho" but instead she said, "I sure will". She hung up the phone and shook off the feeling of disgust. The nerve of some people she thought. After heading off the problem in the restaurant she called Kris to verify his schedule for the week. He was heading to Denver the next day and Sydni needed to type up his itinerary.

She finished up the scheduling made a few calls and was about to go to lunch when she saw Larue's Range Rover pull up. "What the hell?" A few weeks ago I never saw his ass, now he is around all the time. She watched him get out and go to the complex. As soon as she was sure he was in, she made a mad dash to her car. This doesn't make sense, she thought.

The rest of the day went by smoothly. Marc came in after lunch but he really didn't have much to say to Sydni. This was fine for her. She liked it that way. Lillian never made it in that was okay too with Sydni.

Thank goodness for long weekends Sydni thought as she went to Party City to pick up some birthday decorations. It was Memorial Day weekend and Mama's birthday fell on the holiday. Every year they gave her a barbecue/birthday party. Blake was in charge of getting the liquor. Sydni was in charge of decorations. Ariel was cooking, and Mya sending out the invitations. Paige and Rimy were busy straightening out the backyard and getting the garage all cleaned. Zo had already cut the grass so the yard was looking nice. The theme this year was a "Hawaiian Luau." The girls had invited all their friends and all of Mama's closest friends. Every year the party seemed to get bigger.

CHAPTER 8

Sydni was riding past Jam Sounds when she saw Trevor standing next to a pretty red Cadillac. She started to stop but kept going instead. She was so intrigued by him. Sydni had never been afraid to confront a situation, but he made her feel funny. Maybe it was the challenge. He wasn't all over her like most guys. She decided she would approach him Monday at the Paradise.

She pulled up in front of Mya's house and noticed an unfamiliar car in the driveway. She honked her horn and got out and went to the door. He heart almost stopped when she saw Big Darius sitting in her living room. It was too late for her to turn and leave because he had already seen her. She remembered that she was unarmed and that unnerved her even more. "Oh well, I guess I had it coming sooner or later." She thought as she stepped into the house.

"What's up Sydni"? Darius asked.

Even though she was scared as hell she still was mad at him for what he did to Mya. She walked right past him to the back of the house where Mya was.

"What the hell is he doing here? Have you called the Police"? She asked Mya.

"Sydni it's alright. Darius and I have talked it over and he knows that I don't want to be with him anymore, but he still wants to have a relationship with Little Darius". She said.

"Well that's up to you, I guess. What are you wearing to the Party"?

"I don't know yet. Have you heard from Trevor? She asked.

"No, but I just saw him up at Jam Sounds, but I didn't stop."

"What's up with that timid role"? Mya asked.

"Just because I'm not jumping his bones, doesn't mean that I'm timid. Plus he has too many females on him in that club. I noticed a few of them hating on me lately. I don't want to have to mess somebody up about no brotha".

"You're tripping Sydni! You know you want his ass, take him". Mya said.

"You're the one tripping letting that sorry as brotha back in here. He couldn't ever darken my doorstep after that shit". Sydni regretted it before she finished saying it. Mya's face darkened.

"Sydni this is my house and I let whoever the hell I want come over here. You act like you haven't ever made a bad decision before. You are not perfect, even though you would like to believe so. I'm tired of your ass judging me!" Screamed Mya.

"Mya I'm sorry. I didn't mean to say that. You know that stuff is untrue. I would never judge you. You are right this is your house and you have the right to have whomever you want in it".

"And I don't think I want you here right now"! Said Mya.

"Mya, I said I'm sorry". Sydni said.

122

"Leave Sydni".   -   "Look, I think you are blowing this out of proportion Mya." Darius said as he walked into the room. "Sydni has a right to feel the way she feels about me. She is only trying to protect her friend. I am happy that you have been as forgiving as you've been or else I might not be able to save the relationship between my son and I. Out of all of your friends, Sydni has always been there for you through thick and thin, even when I didn't want her to be. She loves you a great deal and I had three cracked ribs to prove it. Give her a chance"!

Sydni couldn't believe her ears. This was not the same person that she had held a gun on. She didn't know where he had been for the last 8 months, but he had definitely made a change for the better. Mya still looked kind of pissed, but she came over and gave Sydni a hug and they apologized to each other. Sydni also thanked Darius for his positive input. He accepted and apologized for what had happened. He explained that he had spent some time in the "Halfway House" and taken some anger management classes. He said that he was still taking a course now. He explained that he needed the classes like an alcoholic needs AA or a gambler needs GA. Sydni was really impressed. It took a big man to admit that he needed help and to actually get it.

After Mya sent Little Darius off with his dad, she and Sydni set off for Mama's house. Sydni asked Mya if she had planned on inviting her new friend to the party. Jermaine was a guy that Mya had met at the Bar. They had been seeing each other every day since they had met. Mya told her yes, that she was bringing him.

"Girl, at first I wasn't going to because we've been seeing so much of each other. I thought I would give us some space but he started tripping when he heard me mention the party. He kept saying I was trying to duck him"! Said Mya.

"What? Already"? Sydni said.

"Yeah, but that's okay, I kind of like the attention". She said. Sydni made sure that she didn't say what she was thinking this time. I just hope that attention doesn't turn into negative attention. She thought.

Blake had just arrived at Mama's house when Sydni and Mya got there. They helped her unload the liquor.

"Eric, go ask Zo to empty out those coolers for the beer and pop." Sydni said. Eric scampered off inside the house. Rimy came outside to show off her new haircut.

"Gone girl"! Said Blake. −"When did you do that"? Sydni asked. "Yesterday". Rimy replied. Her shoulder bob was too cute. She looked well over her 15 years of age. It seemed like over the past year she had blossomed from the tomboy stage everyone thought she would never get over. Her breasts were growing and it seemed like they weren't going to stop! She had gone from an "A" cup to a "C" in about 6 months. Sydni kept her eyes wide open when it came to her little sister. She paid attention to the signs. She would know exactly when to pop the question about the pill. She almost felt guilty about what had happened to Paige, and she wasn't going to let it happen again.

"Sydni let me use your car to go to the store". Rimy asked.

"I don't think so. You don't have license yet". Sydni said. "Quit acting funny, you let me drive any other time". Rimy said.

"Yeah, when I'm in the car." Sydni said. - "Come on Sydni I'll be right back it's only down the street". Said Rimy. "Rimy, you better bring your ass right back. I'm not playing"! Sydni stated. She knew she would regret it later as she handed over the keys to her younger sister. "We drink too much". Sydni laughed as they went into the house. "I will not butt in, I will not butt in, she thought to herself".

After everyone had a Mike's lemonade in their hand. Sydni proposed a toast to the greatest mother in the world. For the rest of the day they all lounged around the house.

The weekend slipped away and finally Monday arrived. It was a beautiful sunny day. It had reached 78 degrees by 3 o'clock. The party was just getting started. Everyone was mingling around and people were still arriving. Mama was looking extra happy carrying around her cup of absolute and orange juice. She had on the outfit that Sydni bought her. It was a pair of blue jean Guess shorts and a Guess T-shirt. Paige had bought her a pair of K-Swiss classics and you couldn't tell her anything. Blake invited her mother Simone. She brought her husband Jack. Mya was sitting at a table with Little Darius and Jermaine. She looked like she was enjoying herself, So Sydni decided not to worry about her. A few of the people from the street had also come down.

Ariel was playing DJ for the day and she was jamming. If they weren't dancing they were bobbing their heads. Rimy was still mad at the world so she was off on the sideline looking mad. Sydni went over to her and started dancing in front of her.

"Go Rimy, go Rimy"! Gone...Sydni, I don't feel like playing". She said.

"Look girl, ain't no sense in being mad, take your punishment like a woman and get over it. Nobody told your ass to take a joyride in my car. So how you gonna be mad at somebody"? Sydni replied.

Rimy rolled her eyes at Sydni and asked her to sneak her a sip of her Mike's lemonade. Sydni poured her some in a cup. She knew she was wrong but Rimy wasn't going anywhere, so what the hell?

The party was going on strong and everybody seemed to be having a lot of fun. Mya, Jermaine, Paige and Zo were playing Spades. While Blake, Ariel and Jay were playing dominoes. In another section of the yard, they had a Tunk game going on at one table and a poker game going at another one. The neighbors, the Simpsons, had gotten into an argument because Mrs. Simpson said Mr. Simpson was looking at Blake too hard. It was hilarious! The girls were jumping double dutch in the driveway and the boys were playing football in a far end of the backyard. It was a perfect party everyone was enjoying themselves, especially Mama, which was most important.

They had agreed that they were gonna take Mama to the Paradise, but she reneged in the end stating that she was going to hang out with some people her own age and get her groove on. "Well excuse us. Go get your groove on". Ariel exclaimed.

Sydni paid Rimy $20 to keep Eric. That must have been the final payback for Sydni getting her in trouble. Sydni was on a mission. She had the perfect dress set out, all she had to do was shower and get ready.

When she finished showering she lotioned up and sprayed herself with her favorite perfume, Chloe Narcisse. Then she put on her dress. She had gone to Status the day before and picked it out, it was a light green dress. It was fitting! She knew she looked like a million bucks and she felt like it too.

They all met up over Ariel's house and went to the club from there. Because it was a holiday plus one of the Club's hyped days, it was jammed packed. Sydni saw a few guys that she knew who let them sit at their table.

Sydni had left her cell phone in her car so she and Mya ran outside to get it. When they came back in she saw Trevor in the Poolroom. He saw her too and motioned for her to come in there. She told Mya she would catch up with her in a minute

The Poolroom was a lot quieter in a separate room from the Club. There were a few guys shooting pool on the opposite table. Trevor was playing against some guy they called Calvin. It was Calvin's turn to shoot so Trevor walked up and hugged Sydni. She reciprocated hugging him back a little longer than normal. He noticed and held her a little tighter.

"What's up with you"? He asked.

"I miss you". Sydni said.

Calvin asked Trevor if he was still playing. He finally let her go. Sydni was about to leave and let him finish his game when he asked her to stay. After he finished the game they walked out to the bar. Trevor ordered a bottle of Christal Champagne. He got two flutes and poured her some. Her friends were spread all over the club dancing or talking to guys. She noticed a few women giving her nasty looks, but they knew better than to make a move. Occasionally Trevor would get caught up in a conversation with a guy, but he would always look around to make sure that Sydni was still standing there.

Up pops Ariel out of nowhere. "So what you just dumped us tonight, huh"? She asked.

"No, never that". Sydni said. Before she could get another word out a Rachelle Farelle song came on and Sydni and Trevor headed straight to the dance floor. For a brief moment there was no one in the club but the two of them. They danced until the song was over. He then told her that he had to leave for a minute, but he would be right back. "Don't leave Sydni"! He said.

"I'm not". She replied.

"And don't be letting these brothas be all in your face either". Trevor commented.

"Come on now". Said Sydni.

As soon as Trevor walked out the door three different guys tried to hit on Sydni. It's amazing how brothas are, she thought to herself. She saw Trevor's friend Jalil pull one of the guys to the side and say something to him. The guy didn't look Sydni's way again. "I wonder what that was all about?" She asked Ariel.

"I don't know but he doesn't look happy, does he"? Ariel said.

Several hours had passed. It was a quarter to two and Trevor still hadn't made it back. Sydni was getting ready to leave not really feeling good about being stood up a good part of the night waiting for him. She was waiting on her car in valet when he pulled up.

"Where are you going"? He asked.

"Home Trevor, where do you think?" She answered with some attitude. Blake and Ariel were still standing there waiting on their car. Mya was kicking it with a guy at the door.

"Have one of them drive your car home and we'll pick it up in the morning". Trevor said. Her mind was telling her no, but her body was telling her yes. She sided with her body.

Sydni asked Mya to drive her car over to Ariel's house and she would be back to get it. All of her friends were giving her the look, but she ignored them. Tonight was the night!

When they pulled into her parking structure, she showed the guard her badge and he let them in. They parked on the fifth floor and got on the elevator to the sixth floor. When they stepped into the courtyard, Trevor was stunned.

"Damn, bay. This is a whole 'nother world up here".
Sydni smiled and enjoyed the moment. She was hoping that he would be really impressed, and he was. When she opened the door to her apartment Trevor looked around like a kid in a candy store.

"You sure you live by yourself"? He asked.

"Why, is that so hard to believe"? Sydni asked.

"My bad, this is just sweet as hell"! Trevor said.

"Thank you--- let me give you a tour".

She gave him the quickie tour of the downstairs and then showed him Eric's room. Sydni saved the best for last...her bedroom. Her king-size bed looked so inviting. It didn't take long before they began to kiss and slowly undress each other. Trevor laid her down and kissed her, he then kissed her breast.

What Sydni had been waiting for and dreaming of had finally come true. This went on for what seemed like hours. The next morning she woke up late for work. She told Trevor she would be back on her lunch hour and then he could take her to get her car. He mumbled "O.K." and went back to sleep.

Sydni could hardly do her work for thinking about the events of the evening. She was literally floating with a smile chisled on her face.

When she got back to the apartment Trevor was still asleep. "Baby get up! I only have an hour".

Trevor got up but not before Sydni noticed his a.m. erection. She walked over and kissed his chest and everywhere else. Before she knew it they were making love again. After their quickie, they jumped in the shower and were pretty close to making love again until Sydni remembered she had to go back to work. Trevor promised he would pick her up from work so she could get her car.

When she got back to work she had three voicemail messages. The first one was from Ariel: "Where the hell are you? Don't tell me we are gonna have to do a 187 on Trevor's ass! If you don't call me or show your face within the hour, I'm calling the Police! You better had had some fun and I want to hear about it! Call me!" The next one was from Mya: "Girl, I know you fucked him. I know you did! Don't try to call me with that goody-two-shoes shit. My money is firmly placed on the bet that you got your groove on last night. And you are being stingy with the story! Call me!" I have some crazy ass friends Sydni thought.

130

Sydni was busy typing up the summer menu when her line rang. "This is Sydni speaking".

"Baby, I forgot to tell you, some brotha named Larue called this morning. I told him don't call back".

"Excuse me.....Trevor you answered my phone"?

"Yeah it was ringing"! He said.

"You had no right to answer my phone. I'm the only person that pays that bill". She replied agitated.

"I left three hundred dollars on the kitchen counter because I had a feeling your smart mouthed ass was gonna say that. Now I pay the bill". Trevor stated.

Sydni cleared her throat and said: "That was still wrong! I'll see you in a minute." She hung up. Sydni didn't know whether she should be happy or mad. Well at least she was rid of Larue. After she called her friends back and filled them in on every detail, she waited patiently for five o'clock to come.

The work- day finally came to an end and Trevor picked Sydni up as planned. He informed her that he had a few runs to make before he took her to get her car. She had no objections as she sank down in the plush seats of his Cadillac. Their first stop was to a Convalescent Home.

"Who is in here"? Sydni asked.

"Trevor's face saddened when he said, "my grandfather".

"I'm sorry! Are you two close"? She asked.

"Yeah, he is the only person who gives a damn about me. I lived with him and my grandmother when I was younger".

He was only gone for about ten minutes. When he got back he was in a very somber mood. Sydni didn't pry. After they made a few more stops she became agitated as hell. She was tired of waiting in the car for him while he took anywhere from 5 minutes to 25 minutes to do whatever he was doing. He noticed that she had an attitude so he decided it was time to drop her off. They agreed to call each other later on.

Ariel was still at work when Sydni picked up her car, so she went straight to daycare to get Eric. She took him to the mall with her to pick out a few pairs of shorts and some new gym shoes with the three hundred dollars that she had thanks to Trevor. She then went to Bennigan's in Southfield for dinner.

Sydni was trying to get Eric to eat his chicken fingers when he surprised her with a question: "Mommy where is Mike"?

Sydni thought long and hard before she answered. "Baby, mommy and Mike are not friends anymore. So I found a new house for you and I. Mike lives in our old house." Very well put, if I must say so myself, she thought.

"Was he mean to you"? He asked.

Breathe, breathe, she told herself. "Well, sometimes he was but you know I am a big girl and I can take care of myself". Whew! She let out a deep breath.

"Well, if anybody is ever mean to you mommy, you can tell me and I will beat them down." Said Eric. The expression on his face said the same. Sydni wasn't surprised

Eric had always been very protective of all the women in his life.

"Well, E I will let you know if that ever happens again and we can beat them down together, okay"? He agreed and finished his chicken fingers. He is such a little man, she thought.

After they finished dinner. Eric made Sydni promise she would watch Hercules with him. So when they got home Eric got in bed with her and snuggled. He was sleep before the previews finished. She got up to straighten her room, her dress was still draped over her chair. She picked it up and placed it in the dry cleaning bag. Then she went into the bathroom and put Trevor's washcloth and bath towel in the hamper. She put up the toothbrush he had used. Trevor was weighing heavily on her mind she started to call him, but decided against the idea. Let him call me, she thought. Sydni fell asleep waiting for the phone to ring.

Even though they had not made a formal commitment, it was common knowledge in the Paradise that Trevor and Sydni were a couple. Not too many guys dared to talk to Sydni anymore. The few that didn't know were usually put in check as soon as they stepped to her. Sydni had in fact checked a few women about Trevor. But, she was getting tired of the games. This was unlike her. She was at the bar twice a week sometimes three times. She was tired of girls hating her for no reason. Trevor was not her man. She couldn't help it that he would be kicking with them and as soon as she walked in the bar, he wouldn't speak anymore.

Things always have a way of working themselves out. Finally one day Sydni and Blake had gone to the bar and were sitting down talking when they noticed Trevor walking out the door with a light skinned girl. Sydni who had already had a few too many drinks in her, followed them out the door. She called to Trevor who told her he would be right back. Sydni was steaming as she told him to come to her. He kept walking. The girl looked at her and grinned. Sydni's ego was shot. She couldn't believe that he had still gone with the girl after she had come outside to get him. Blake who had followed Sydni outside told her to forget about him. She asked the valet to get her car.

The valet came back with the car and Sydni was about to leave when Trevor came running up.

"Where are you going"? He asked.

"Leave her alone Trevor"! Said Blake.

"What is wrong with you? I was only walking her to her car." He said.

"Well how come when I said come here, you kept walking? Who is she Trevor"?

"That's just my friend". He said.

"All the time we have been kicking it, I have never disrespected you in this club. What you did was totally disrespectful. Are you fucking her too"?

What he said next, made both Sydni and Blake's heads turn.

"Yeah, but she ain't nobody". He said.

Sydni turned the ignition and drove off. When they pulled up in front of Blake's house she put her head down on the steering wheel and cried. She cried for every bad experience that she'd had over the past year and a half. Blake decided she needed to stay over and guided her into the house and helped her lie down on the couch. She slept for a few hours and then went to pick up Eric from Mama's house.

The next couple of months went by like a blur at work. Sydni was so emotionally numb that she barely noticed the things that Marc, Lillian, and the new Marketing Manager Wanda were doing. Her duties were so minimal now that they had hired Wanda that she was basically staring at a blank computer screen most of the day. If they found some menial task for her to do, she would complete it and go back to her desk. The only time she was vibrant was when she talked to Kris. She had put her all in planning his family's Christmas vacation. Even though they still had a month before they left, Sydni was making sure that everything was perfect. At the end of the day she went home and laid down.

Holidays were always special to the Jamison family. Everyone was getting ready the upcoming one. Sydni's aunt Maxine was cooking Thanksgiving Dinner. And boy could she cook! They were having honey baked ham, turkey, macaroni and cheese, greens, coleslaw, chitterlings, candy yams, stuffing and cranberry sauce. Sydni expected that she would be putting on a few pounds this week. She had actually lost a few after the incident with Trevor. After she stopped going to the bar it seemed like her energy had returned. She promised herself that she would get over him. He called a few times after that, but she never returned his calls. Sydni knew there was a reason that she didn't want to kick it with him. She promised herself that she would follow her first mind from now on.

Thanksgiving was beautiful everyone ate a lot, played cards, and danced. The group began to get sleepy and pooped out about 6 o'clock. Sydni took Eric home and turned in early.

135

The Christmas holiday was approaching fast. The girls wanted to take Sydni out for her birthday, and of course they had to go the Paradise. She hadn't been there in over two months and she definitely didn't miss it. She was afraid that she would run into that girl that she had acted a fool in front of.

Blake said: "Don't worry about that shit. If she has anything to say about it then we'll just beat her ass and be done with this place". When Sydni walked in everyone screamed, "surprise". The girls had planned a surprise party for her! Everyone was there, even Mama! Sydni was so happy that she didn't notice Trevor walk in. They ordered a tray of Tequila shots. She went to work on them. Sydni was having a great time until she saw Trevor over by the DJ staring at her while she danced by herself. She kept dancing and rolled her eyes at him. He seemed unmoved he just kept staring at her.

After the song went off she went back to the table. Blake was elbowing Jay in the arm because he was nodding off to sleep. Mama was looking bored. Sydni had collected five hundred dollars on her shirt and was pretty drunk. She told them that she was ready if they were. They gathered up her balloon bouquet and presents and were about to leave when Trevor walked up and said. "Sydni aren't you gonna introduce me to your mom"?

Sydni rolled her eyes and walked away. Ariel made the introduction and walked out after Sydni.

"Can you believe him?" Asked Sydni.

"Frankly, yes I can. That's just how he is Sydni". She said.

This had to be the worst winter Michigan had seen since the seventies. They had received three feet of snow and the roads were bad, which was why Sydni was pissed that she had to drive Kris and his son and daughter to the airport. Here they are on their way to Hawaii, and I have to trudge through this bullshit to take them to the damn airport, she thought.

Kris's daughter Emily promised to bring Sydni a coconut bra and a grass skirt back.

"Thanks Emily, I've always wanted a coconut bra". Sydni said.

Once she saw them off, she made her way back home. The Brewery was closed due to the weather and Sydni was glad. She rarely had anything to do anyway, so she went home to clean up and wash some clothes. She also wanted to finish up Eric's Christmas shopping. She had already bought too much stuff she thought, but she kept seeing things that she wanted him to have.

There was a message from Big Eric asking her to call him when she got in. His line was busy the first time that she tried. She finally got through the second time.

"What's up E"? She asked.

"Sydni I wanted to know if I could stay over tomorrow night to wake up with Eric on Christmas"?

"Eric, you haven't been waking up with him on Christmas. If this is some sorry ass excuse to try to get over and get in my bed, don't even think about it.

"Bay, you know I love you but don't flatter yourself. I'm for real. It would mean a lot to me and I think it would mean a lot to little man too".

"Well, maybe you are right. I'll think about it and let you know. I'm not trying to give him some false hope that you and I are getting back together".

"I understand, well let me know". They hung up.

She finished her shopping and she and Eric baked cookies that night. Sydni had Christmas Eve off work, so she stayed up late and watched scary movies.

Sydni decided to let Big Eric stay over. The next day was Christmas Eve so he came over around seven and they went and had egg nog and drinks over Mama's house.

Rimy and Paige were giving Sydni the look, but she was ignoring them.

When they got back to Sydni's house it was already nine thirty. Eric was anxious to go to sleep so he could wake up to his presents. They ate some of their home baked cookies with milk. Sydni finally gave in and let him go to sleep. Big Eric took him upstairs and tucked him in.

The two of them watched a movie, after that they talked and laughed until two o'clock. Sydni made sure Eric was sleep they then put his toys under the tree.

"This is the last year I'm gonna let him believe in Santa. I don't want my son believing some fat White man is sneaking in his house and bringing him presents, when we work our asses off to go into debt every year for his little butt." Big Eric said.

"Who said he believes Santa is White? Eric is at a stage in his life where he doesn't know color. If you ask him what color he is, he will say brown. Ask him what color I am, and he'll say peach. He doesn't see in black and white. And to correct you on something you said earlier. We don't do anything, I work my ass off to buy him stuff!" She said.

"Why do you always have to throw that in my face? I know I haven't been the best father financially, but you know I've been there in every other aspect." He said.

"I'm sorry Eric, I always know how to ruin a good time, don't I"? Sydni said.

"That's okay, so where am I sleeping"? He asked.

"Right here." She said as she patted the couch. She gave him some blankets and a pillow and went upstairs. She changed into her most unattractive pair of flannel pajamas and got in bed. Sydni thought about the old days when she and Eric were together and she almost took a back slide. She went downstairs to get a cup of water and saw that he was still up. He joked about her pajamas and she went back upstairs. "I'm just lonely, she thought. I just want to be held." She pulled the covers up to her chin and fell asleep.

Little Eric was extra happy to see both of his parents on Christmas morning. Sydni told Eric thanks for a good idea.

After they were dressed, Big Eric left. Sydni promised to bring the baby over to his grandmother's house later. Once she had packed the car up with all the gifts and everything that Eric refused to leave at home, she headed to her aunt Sarah's house for breakfast. It was tradition that they held breakfast as Sarah's and dinner at Mama's every year.

When they arrived, Mama was just pulling up too. Paige and Rimy grabbed all the packages and walked to the door. Grandma Sally opened the door for them and they were immediately overwhelmed by the smells of bacon and sausage. Sydni's dad was in the kitchen throwing down. After breakfast everyone exchanged gifts. They then sat around for a while talking. Everyone started yawning, the sign that it was time to go to Mama's to lie down for a while. After they said their good-byes the girls went home.

At dinner all of her mother's relatives came over and they exchanged their gifts. Sydni thought to herself. "This holiday is beginning to be so overrated." She could only imagine how much had been spent just on the kids. She knew she had spent a mint on Little Eric and with the gifts she had bought her sisters and mom, she would have to work a few hours overtime to replace what she had spent. Next year I am not doing this. She vowed to whoever was listening.

"That's what you said last year". Mama said.

"I know, I'm just talking". Said Sydni.

Rimy came and gave her a hug thanking her for the gift she gave her. Sydni had bought both of her sisters Coach purses with matching wallets. She had also given Rimy a beautiful gold bracelet. Paige had asked for clothes so she got her a pair of Polo jeans with a long sleeve Polo tee. Mama was ecstatic about her Spa package. She would be getting a 1 1/2 hour massage, pedicure, manicure and facial. Mama loved stuff like that so Sydni always tried to indulge her for her birthday and Christmas. Everyone was happy so that automatically made Sydni happy. Maybe it was all worth it, she thought. Nah!

Sydni had planned a New Years Eve bash at the apartment. Little Eric always went to church with his dad's grandmother, so that made her free for the night. She had bought everybody's favorite drink plus a few bottles of Moet. Blake and Ariel were burning the wingdings in the kitchen. Mya and Sydni were doing the last minute clean up.

Shawntel and her husband were the first to arrive. They brought a friend from their church with them whose name was Johnny. All four of the girls were eyeing him. He was fine, that was until he opened his mouth. He had a very squeaky annoying little voice. It was a shame because his body was nowhere near little. Oh well! They all thought what a waste.

Second Time ... Shame On Me.

CHAPTER 9

Mya's guy Jermaine came next. He and Mya had officially become a couple a few months before. Sydni hadn't noticed anything fishy going on and Mya seemed happy, so she had set her premonitions from earlier that year, to the side. He also brought his friend Gerald with him. Mya showed them in and took their coats. Blake and Jay were arguing as usual in the kitchen. Sydni slid between them and told them to chill.

"Do you guys want to start your New Year out on a bad note? Besides you're embarrassing me in front of our guests!" She said as she walked away.

Blake's brother Donald and one of his many freaks showed up next. Donald was a straight up ladies man. Sydni had never seen him with the same woman twice. It didn't help that he was a male stripper! Ariel had invited her new friend Lance and he showed up with a bottle of Jack Daniels. The party was jumping! The music was pumping and they had Dick Clark's rocking New Year's Eve on the television on mute. Everyone was enjoying themselves. Sydni had started a Soul Train line and was doing the German Smurf when Ariel handed her the phone. It was Big Eric he was calling to wish her a happy New Year.

"Sydni I know something has been going on with you for the last couple of months. But I just want you to know that I think you are the best thing that has ever happened to me and I thank the Lord every day that you are the mother of my child. I couldn't ask for a better baby momma, even though you trip on me sometimes. If you ever reconsider what we could have together, I know our future would be bright. If you don't then I'm satisfied with the relationship that we have now."

Sydni was stunned. "Thank you Eric for all the compliments, but you know I think it's best that we remain friends for our son's sanity. I don't know what the future holds for us." She said. "There you go with that crap. Happy New Year Sydni". He said. "Happy New Year Eric". Said Sydni.

"Hey everybody! The ball is about to drop". Said Mya. 7-6-5-4-3-2-1—"HAPPY NEW YEAR". They all screamed. Sydni felt a pang of envy as all of her friends hugged and kissed their mates. Johnny started walking towards her but turned away when she gave him the "Don't even think about it look!" After they all made a toast to the New Year Donald put on a show for the Ladies. They played charades and it was well into the morning before everyone started going home. Jermaine told Sydni that it was a great party and they would have to do it again soon. Sydni looked around her apartment and said. "Not too soon." She had a mess to clean up. The girls promised to come over the next day and help her clean up but she told them it was alright she had it covered. Much to her chagrin Sydni found herself alone again.

She started to pick up the noisemakers and Tiara's and hats they had been wearing. She gathered all the cups and bottles and threw them in the garbage. Mama would kill her if she knew. She was a stickler for saving the 10-cent deposit on bottles. She could hear her now. "You must be rich". She laughed to herself and took the garbage to the chute. She was tired as hell she just didn't want to get into the bed alone. She finished straightening up and finally went to bed. "Please don't let my New Year be like this"! She prayed.

144

The following morning when she arrived at work and checked her voicemail for messages from Kris, he had said that he was due to return on Wednesday. She couldn't wait to hear about the trip. While she was checking, Marc motioned for her to get off the phone and meet him in his office. She hung up the phone and went into his office.

"Shut the door behind you". Marc said. "Oh brother Sydni thought".

"Sydni I brought you in here to let you know that we no longer need your services here. We didn't do as well as we thought we would this first year and the budget doesn't allow any room for your salary. Besides we really don't need an Office Manager because the girls pretty much can handle everything themselves".

Sydni looked him square in his eyes and told him. "You miserable excuse for a man. You don't even have enough guts to out and out fire me. Marc, kiss my ass, and I mean every last inch of it". With that she went and got her coat and purse and threw the keys on the desk. Before she left she went over to Lillian's desk and said. "If you were twenty years younger I would beat your ass, but instead I'll just put in a call to your husband and let him know Marc's dick is in your mouth." She pushed over the hot steaming cup of coffee that was on Lillian's desk. She watched as the black liquid soaked into all the documents she had on her desk. She didn't wait for a response as she walked away.

When Sydni got to the house she kicked off her shoes, threw her head in her hands and willed herself not to cry. "Stop feeling sorry for yourself dammit." She said out loud. She then turned on the TV and the "Jerry Springer Show" was just coming on. The episode was called "Honey I'm Leaving You For Your Mother." She flipped through the channels and came back to the "Springer Show". "I might as well watch some people that have a more dysfunctional life than my own." She thought as she drifted off to sleep. She woke up to the phone ringing.

"Hello". She said. – "What's this about, you no longer work at the Brewery"? Asked Mama. "I just called there and that's what they said".

"I don't Mama, Marc fired me today! Mama I really don't feel like talking about it right now. So I'll call you back".

"Okay, but you know if you need me, I got your back". Mama said.

"I know, thanks Ma". She hung up the phone and went back to sleep.

The next day she went down to the Unemployment Agency and filed. She also put in a call to Blake to see if her In-Laws needed any help with their number business. There were three families that monopolized the "Street Lottery" and they were one of them. Luckily they had a space open. She agreed to start that day at 4:30pm. She had filled in for a few girls that had gone on vacation in the past, so she didn't need training. She also called Tony at the Bar and asked him if she could have her days back at the Bar. He gladly accepted her back. He had gone through three barmaids since she had left. "Street Life, It's The Only Life I Know". She sang to herself.

Later that day she went to the grocery store and picked up Eric before it was time for her to go to the Number House. She also went to Cellular One and lowered her plan to a cheaper one. She wasn't planning on being broke if she could help it.

When she got to work Mama and Blake were already there. Mama assigned her a "Book" that she would be responsible for every week. The night went smoothly and she even hit the lottery! They were finished by 8 o'clock and Sydni was home by 8:15pm. "I think I can handle this". She said to herself.

Sydni had been officially unemployed for one week and had gained three pounds. During the day she found herself eating and watching TV. Then when she got to the Number House all they did was snack and sit on their butts for four hours.

"I've got to slow down. I'm gonna be as big as the house if I keep this up". Sydni told Blake.

"If anybody knows, you know it's me. What's up for the night?" Asked Blake

"Shit, the baby is over his dad's, so I figured I'd have a blockbuster night." Sydni replied. "I heard that". Said Blake.

"I'll call you when I get home, Mama". Sydni said as she got into her car. When she got home she took a bath and popped herself some popcorn and put the movie "Love Jones" in the VCR. Blake called in the middle of the movie.

"Sydni, I don't think I can take this shit anymore, I know you've heard me say it over and over again, but I'm serious this time. He stole my baby's tuition money. It's one thing to steal from me but not my kids."

'I'm sorry Blake, that is a messed up situation. You've stuck it out a lot longer than I think I could have. You need to keep in mind that you will be thirty in a few years and I know you don't want to be going through this shit then. I

147

don't have a lot of space but you are welcome to come over here if you want to." Said Sydni.

"No Sydni I talked to my grandmother and she said that I could come over there. You know her basement is finished and it's big as hell. But you are right about that shit. I don't want to still be battling with him when I'm thirty". Said Blake.

"So how are you holding up?" Asked Blake. – I'm fine, I like the peace and quiet". Sydni lied. "Actually I'm lying, she said. I'm miserable and horny as hell. How come I can't have a relationship like these two". Sydni asked referring to the couple in the movie. " I have yet to meet a man who will cook me breakfast".

"Girl I think that's only in the movies, brothas ain't shit". Said Blake. Just then Sydni's line clicked. "Hold on Blake. Hello".

"Are you pregnant"? Who the hell is this? Sydni asked.

"So you don't know my voice now"? - "Whoever this is, you're about to get hung up on because I don't have time for these games". Sydni said.

"It's Trevor". He said.

Is that all you could come up with for an excuse to call me? You and I haven't fucked in some months and if I was pregnant that problem would have been taken care of right away.

"It's like that Sydni". He said.

"Yes, it's like that Trevor. Now I'd appreciate it if you would state your business because I have someone on the other line".

"Who"? He asked.

"Trevor that's none of your business!

"Okay, I want to talk to you". He said.

"Well, go ahead and talk". She said.

"No, I mean face to face". He replied.

"Why should I"? She asked.

"Sydni can you do it for me, please"?

"Well, we are taking Blake out for her birthday tomorrow and we are meeting at the bar for a minute." She said.

"What time"? Trevor asked.

"Around nine". Sydni indicated. – "I'll be there". Trevor said and hung up.

Sydni clicked back over. She was surprised that Blake had held on so long. "You're not going to believe this".

The next day after work they all met up at the bar. It was a quarter to nine by that time. They all ordered a drink. The bar was relatively empty except for the ballroom instructor and a few students. Blake was the only one that knew Trevor was suppose to be coming there and Sydni noticed her watching the clock.

149

At nine o'clock on the nose Trevor walked through the door. Sydni's heart skipped a beat. He came over to their table and spoke to everyone. He grabbed Sydni by the hand. In passing he told the waitress to get the table another round of drinks. Trevor literally pulled Sydni into the Poolroom and sat her down in a chair.

"Where are y'all going"? Trevor asked.

"None of your business, Trevor". What do you want to talk about because you only have a few minutes". Said Sydni.

"I miss you Sydni". You know I'm not good at this, so bear with me. I'm sorry for whatever I did to make you that mad at me. You do realize I haven't talked to you in a couple of months, don't you"? He said.

"Yes, I do". She said.

"You sure do know how to hold a grudge". Said Trevor.

"That's one thing you will learn about me. So what are you getting at Trevor'? Asked Sydni.

"I miss you and I want to start over". He stated.

"Well let me think about it and I'll give you a call". She said.

"See there you go bullshitting again". He said.

"Or I don't have to call you at all. Trevor if I'm going to do this it's gonna be on my terms, not yours.". Said Sydni.

150

"All right, but don't take too long. – And call me when you get in the house tonight". Trevor said.

Sydni looked at him and shook her head. "Maybe". She said as she walked back to the table.

She couldn't wipe the grin off her face. Blake noticed as she walked up. She didn't say anything because Trevor was watching her from the door. They finished their drinks and got up to leave. When they passed the Poolroom Trevor was shooting pool by himself. Sydni waved good-bye and he waved back and tapped his watch. She laughed and walked out the door.

They were going to see the strippers and had reserved a table right next to the stage. Mya had picked up her cake, which was shaped like a giant penis. It had a straw in the middle that Blake was suppose to suck on to get the surprise liquid out! They were all having a ball. Ariel was getting a lap dance by a dancer named "Midnight". She looked like she was in love. Mya was busy with "Snap". This man was not a looker but he had a straight up six pack and legs like a horse! Blake had two guys rolling around in front of her! Sydni was getting a dance from a very well endowed gentleman by the name of "Chocolate Thunder". His G-string was made like an elephant head, the trunk was extra long. Blake's friend Myesha was whispering in her ear.

"That could not be real". Sydni didn't care at that point. When the song was over the guys retreated back stage. Now it was time for the birthday dances.

The MC placed a chair in the middle of the stage and asked for the birthday girl to come up to the stage. The girls pushed Blake up there and made her sit down. The lights went low and, "Do me" by Prince came over the speakers. From the side of the stage entered the most gorgeous man they had ever seen. Everybody at Blake's table was screaming. The man only had a towel wrapped around his bottom half. He carried a can of whip cream. When he reached Blake he gently rubbed her face and gave her the whipped cream. He instructed her to spray it over his private parts. After Blake had sprayed him really good, he let the towel drop! He danced that way for about two minutes. The crowd was screaming! Blake's face was beet red. He then sprayed a dab of cream on her cleavage and licked it off! When the song was over he wrapped the towel back around him and gave Blake a hug and walked off the stage. Sydni, Ariel, and Mya's mouths were on the floor.

"Oh my God"! Blake kept saying over and over! After that they each got pissy drunk. At the end of the night Blake had to be carried out of the bar.

After Sydni dropped Blake off safely at her grandmother's, she was searching frantically through her purse for Trevor's number. After seeing all those hard bodies. Sydni had to get some! She called his cell phone and told him to meet her down at the apartment. He was there before she was with a big grin on his face.

The next morning he said. "You must have been super horny last night because you put me straight to sleep".

"Yeah I must have been doing some acrobatics because I'm sore as hell". She said.

He asked her why wasn't she going to work? She explained the situation to him. He gave her a thousand dollars and told her to pay what bills she could with that and he would give her some more later if she needed it. He got up and got in the shower. She noticed that he left his T-shirt in the hamper. When he got out Sydni was downstairs nursing her hangover.

"I have some runs to make, but I'll call you a little later". He said. Sydni mumbled a weak "okay" and took down two Advil.

When they got to work, all they could talk about was Blake's birthday surprise. Both Sydni and Blake were still suffering from their hangovers and could barely see to check their numbers. Mama was going off on them telling them that they drank too much and that getting drunk like that wasn't cute. Neither of them dared to argue with her out of respect, and for the simple fact that it hurt to talk. After they finished their work they each walked slowly to their cars and went home.

Thank goodness Big Eric was keeping the baby all week. It probably wouldn't have been a good idea to let him see her like this again, she thought. Heaven forbid he think I was "drinking drugs" again, she giggled to herself. Sydni took a shower and got in the bed. She had just changed her linens and sprayed them with a new linen freshener from Bath and Body Works when she heard the buzzer.

"Who the hell could this be"? She wondered. She went downstairs and checked the monitor it was Trevor.

"Yes". She said. "It's me let me up". Said Trevor. She buzzed him in. When he came up she noticed he was carrying some bags.

"That smells so good". She said. "I stopped at Franklin's and picked us up some soul food". Said Trevor.

"I didn't know you were coming over tonight". Sydni said.

"What? You didn't want me to"? He asked.

153

"I didn't say that. I just hadn't talked to you all day, so I didn't know". She said.

"I told you I had a few runs to make". He said as he pulled two plates down from the cupboard. She made their plates and they took them upstairs and watched TV and ate in bed. After they ate they watched a movie and went to sleep. In the middle of the night Sydni woke up when Trevor put his arm around her waist. "This is too good to be true". she thought and fell back to sleep.

The rest of the week was basically the same. They would wake up together, go their separate ways during the day, sometimes meet for dinner and meet back at the house at night.

Sydni had started working at the bar again. This was her weekend to work. It felt kind of strange being back. Everyone welcomed her back with open arms. It was the usual crew working that night. Sydni and Melanie behind the bar. Mya, Ariel and Blake were on the floor. There was a guest DJ there that night and he was jamming. The club was packed as usual and the crowd was hyped. Sydni was making three orders at a time and her back had started hurting. Mya came over to the waitress stand and was bitching because she couldn't get her drinks out fast enough. About that time Jermaine walked up behind her and planted a kiss on the back of her neck. She turned around with an attitude because she thought he was someone else. Seeing it was him changed her attitude instantly as she smiled. Melanie got her drinks and she and Jermaine walked away. Blake was screaming for three Coronas and twelve Heinekens.

"I hate when that customer of hers comes in". Said Melanie. "Shit, getting 15 beers is easier than pouring 15 drinks". Said Sydni. They slipped past one another and finished their drinks.

"Sydni! Sydni"! "Who the hell is that calling my name like that"? Sydni questioned. She looked to the end of the bar and it was Mya. She looked terrified! "What's wrong"? Sydni asked.

"Maine is tripping! Girl he just checked Rock about talking to me"!

"Rock? Oh no"! Sydni exclaimed.

Rock was a well-known leader of a street gang and Sydni knew he wasn't going to accept being checked by Maine.

"Look Mya, I hate to say it but that is between those two. You stay out of it because I don't want you to get hurt. But I advise you to have Jermaine leave if you know what's good for him".

Jermaine was standing behind her and had heard everything.

"I'm not going anywhere! I got something for that brotha. He shouldn't be disrespecting me like that". Maine said.

"Really Maine, he wasn't saying anything. He is one of my regular customers so yeah we talk a little. He knows about you". Said Mya.

"So now you sticking up for him"? Asked Maine.

"Look y'all I got to go, I got a thousand people calling my name. Maine, maybe you shouldn't come up here if you can't handle seeing her just talk to people, because that's part of her job". Sydni said as she walked away.

Rock must have been in a good mood or something because he and his crew left the bar peacefully. This did wonders for Jermaine's already inflated ego.

"I told y'all that brotha ain't shit".

"Yeah, yeah. I'll be sure to leave five minutes after your ass". Said Sydni as she wiped the bar down.

"Maine you can't just be walking up checking people in here". Melanie chimed in.

"I heard that". Ariel replied. She was sitting at the bar getting her feet rubbed by Lance.

"Must be nice"! Said Sydni.

"Yes it is". Ariel answered.

"Blake would you answer my phone please"! Asked Sydni.

Blake reached in Sydni's purse and pulled out her cell phone. "It's your husband". Said Blake.

Sydni grabbed the phone from her snickering friend. She told Trevor she would be at home in twenty minutes.

"Cracking the whip already is he"? Ariel asked.

"I don't think so ...He's just ready to go to bed". Replied Sydni.

"You haven't given the man a key yet"? Mya asked.

"No because we don't live together". Sydni said.

"Has he met Eric yet"? Melanie asked.

"No, but that's a dragon I'm gonna slay when I get to it". She knew that would be sooner than later because Eric was coming home on Sunday.

When she got home Trevor was asleep in his car on the fifth floor of the structure. She tapped on the window to wake him up. She could tell he was drunk. She helped him out of the car and into the house.

"I can't believe you drove home like this". She said. She helped him take off his clothes and helped him into bed. She then went into the bathroom and got two Advil and a cup of water.

"Here take these or you'll be sorry in the morning". She had a thousand questions to ask him Like: "Where the hell had he been"? But she decided to wait until the morning. She undressed and got in bed.

The weather turned bad over-night leaving a few inches of snow on the ground by the time that Sydni woke up. She decided to ask Trevor if she could drive his car because she didn't feel like fighting the snow with her rear wheel drive car that day. Another impulse buy that was not well thought out, when she saw that big shiny Mustang she had to have it, not realizing what a pain in the ass it would be in the winter.

Trevor's car on the other hand had heated seats and everything. He said that she could drive it.

Sydni had a standing appointment at Mario's every Saturday. Mario's was a unique Salon that catered to both male and female clientele. On the one side of the Salon there was a row of ladies chatting while the Stylist laid their hair out. On the other side was a row of barber chairs filled with men and barbers circling them and chatting as they cut their hair. When Sydni pulled up in front, she decided that she had better park in the lot. "That's all I need is for someone to slide into his car while I have it". She thought.

It was 11 o'clock her standard appointment time. Sydni had been coming to this shop for two years.

"What's up Sydni? Where is Little E"? Asked Mario.

"He's with his dad this week". She said.

"Oh no! I hope he doesn't come back with his hairline pushed back". Said Mario laughing

"I hope he doesn't either". She laughed.

Mario finished the lady in his chair and started on her. Sydni routinely got a shampoo and her hair conditioned. This kept her hair nice and soft and alive. She started this after her hair had started to have spilt ends and was breaking off. They exchanged pleasantries with one another. Then it was time for shoptalk. There was a conversation going on between two of the stylist about a backstabbing friend. There was another conversation going on amongst the barbers and the guys waiting to be cut. They were discussing the difference between White Strip Clubs and Black Strip Clubs. Sydni recognized one of the guys who had a red skullcap on. She recognized him as a regular. He was saying that Black girls get raunchier and were willing to go farther for the dollar. Another guy countered that there were two different types of men going to the bars, so of course there would be different things going on. White sport coats are going to the White Joints. They have better security for the girls and they

158

enforce the "Look but don't touch rule." At the Black Clubs you have some dancers that don't mind being touched so they are making the money. The ones that don't want to be touched are forced to compromise their integrity.

An unheard female voice spoke up. "They have already compromised their integrity by stripping anyway. Also, how do you guys know so much about this subject"? There was a lot of laughter but no volunteers to give an explanation.

Sydni was just listening. She'd heard it all before. This was a popular topic every Saturday after most of the guys had been to one of the clubs the night before. The two other ladies in the shop smiled but made no comment.

"I wish I was guaranteed a ten dollar tip after each drink I serve. I'd be a millionaire". Said Sydni.

"Baby I'll tip you ten dollars. Do you work tonight"? Said the guy with the hat.

"I work the whole weekend. I'll hold you to that". Sydni said. "No problem". Said Red Hat.

Mario whispered in her ears. "You need to quit it".

"I know I can't help it". Sydni said.

When she left the shop she called to check on Trevor. He didn't answer so she assumed that he was still sleep. She called Ariel to see if she wanted to go to IHOP with her, but she had already gone out to eat with Lance.

"You guys are getting pretty serious, don't you think"? Sydni asked.

"We'll talk about that later. But, girl he is hilarious. He has had me cracking up ever since he picked me up". Said Ariel.

"Well I guess I'll go by myself". Said Sydni. She changed her mind when she saw there were no parking spaces left at the IHOP. She stopped at Burger King and got a Whopper Combo. As she pulled out on to Grand River, she thought about going to the $2.00 Carwash, but remembered he went to the hand Carwash. She passed her old High School Redford High. "Boy did I have some good times there". Sydni tried the house one more time. He still didn't answer so she went and picked up Mama and took her to Target, and ended up spending $200 in there.

They had a sale on men's pajamas so she picked up a few pair for Trevor, even though they always ended up naked in the morning.

"What am I doing? She asked herself. Mama asked her the same thing. "Who are those for"? Mama asked.

"Trevor Mama, he's been staying over a lot lately".

"That's funny I hadn't heard you talk about him for a while." Mama said.

"It's a long story, I'll tell you later." She said. They finished shopping and Sydni dropped Mama off at home. After picking up her dry cleaning she went to her place.

Trevor was right where she had left him. She wondered if she should put a mirror under his nose to see if he was alive. He had slept twelve hours straight. She didn't bother him.

Sydni didn't know what to do with this time on her hand and Trevor asleep. After a bit she went downstairs and started reading "Mama" by Terry McMillan. She had already read it once, but she always read her favorite books twice. After reading for a couple of hours she fell asleep.

Sydni was sound asleep, but Trevor's talking on the phone woke her up. He was arguing with someone but she couldn't tell who it was. It really wasn't any of her business, so she tried to go back to sleep. Minutes later he stomped down the stairs and told her he had to leave and he would call her in a minute. She reminded him that she had to work again that night. He said okay and left.

Sydni had to be at work at 4:30Pm so she got up and got dressed. Much to her surprise Trevor was back before she left. He seemed upset so she asked him what was wrong.

He said, "Nothing, I'm just gonna go back to bed".

Sydni was kind of hurt that he didn't want to share his problems with her, but she knew better than to push him.

She told him to make sure he locked the door behind him if he decided to leave. She wasn't sure if he'd heard her because he was already on his way upstairs.

The bar was kind of slow. Sydni didn't know how she did it, but she had managed to get $250 in tips. This was okay though because she had been able to stash yesterday's tips because of the thousand she had gotten from Trevor. She had put half of that up and spent $200 of it at Target. She had paid her utilities and cell phone bill with the remaining three.

Trevor was gone when she got home, so she called and asked him where he was. He told her that he was on his way there. When she hung up she slipped on a new bra and a G-string set she had bought at Victoria's Secret. She lit some candles and went downstairs to see if she still had any wine left.

The phone was ringing so she answered from the extension in the kitchen.

"Hello". Sydni answered

"May I speak to Sherry"? The man said. She instantly recognized the voice it was Trevor on the line.

"What! Who... did you ask for"? She asked, but then she wasn't sure if it was him or not because the voice sounded a little different.

"I asked for Sherry". He said.

I'm sorry you must have the wrong number". Sydni said as she held the phone uncertain of what had just happened. She hung up the phone and redialed Trevor's number, his voicemail popped on the first time so she dialed again. He answered on the second ring. She asked him had he just called the house. He said no. Sydni didn't ask again, she just hung up and went and changed into her flannel pajamas and got under the covers. She got up one more time and blew out the candles. She was definitely not in the mood anymore.

Sydni heard her door buzzer go off. She buzzed the buzzer and didn't wait for him to get to the door. She unlocked the door and went back to bed. He came in and wanted to talk, but she acted like she was sleep. He got the hint and got in the bed and went to sleep.

The next day Trevor could definitely tell that Sydni had an attitude. She was slamming doors and stomping around all morning. Finally after he realized she wasn't going to allow him to get any peaceful sleep. He came downstairs just as she was throwing the teakettle on the stove.

"What is your problem"? He asked.

"Nothing"! She said.

"There is something wrong with you Sydni. So what is it"? He asked.

"Well for starters, I don't appreciate you calling here last night asking to speak to another girl". She said.

"What are you talking about"? He asked.

"You know that was you that called last night. Just admit that you made a mistake and called the wrong number"!

"I didn't call here and ask for someone else". He said.

"You did, but it's obvious that you are not going to admit it. You know I don't ask much of you, but honesty is one thing that I am going to demand. I won't lie to you so I hope you can do the same for me". Sydni said.

"You don't have to move your head like that and have your hands on your hips like that". He said.

She couldn't help but smile. "See you always want to make a joke out of everything". She said as she playfully punched him in the arm.

Trevor came over and put his arms around her waist and kissed her.

"Oh yeah, there is something else we need to discuss". Said Sydni.

"What now"? Asked Trevor.

"Eric is coming home today". She said.

"And"! He asked.

"And, I haven't told him about you yet. I don't want to send my child into shock when he sees a man lying in my bed. It has been just us for a while now and I think he is used to that. Besides if we are not going to stay together, I would rather him not meet you anyway". She said.

"Who said we weren't gonna be together". Asked Trevor.

"I did, if you pull some more shit like last night".

"Stop tripping". He said as he pulled her back towards him. "You wouldn't be mad if I asked you to stay at your apartment tonight"? Sydni asked.

"No, you just better not be pulling no slick shit". He said.

"You got nerve". She snorted and poured them each a glass of juice.

It was a lazy Sunday, Sydni didn't feel like getting up and going over to Mama's, but she had cooked corned beef and cabbage and her stomach wouldn't let her pass.

When she got to Mamas, the crew was already there. Paige went into her act right away.

"Oh you and Ariel want to start acting brand new, now that y'all got some live-in-dick at home".

"Watch your mouth Paige"! Mama said.

"What are you talking about"? Asked Sydni.

"Any other day y'all would have been here by now"! Said Paige.

"Whatever, girl". Sydni replied. Then she turned to Ariel and asked. "Does Lance live with you"?

"Hell no. Paige don't know what she is talking about. She ought to know about live-in-dick though as much as Zo is over here". She said to Ariel.

"Where is Rimy"? Sydni asked.

"She stayed overnight at Tasha's house". Said Paige.

About that time Mya and Blake walked in, they had gone to the store for Mama.

"What's up sleepy head"? Blake asked Sydni.

"I wasn't asleep, I was just lounging around". She replied.

"Is he wearing you out like that"? Mya asked.

"No, why does everything have to do with Trevor"? Sydni asked.

"Well excuse us." Said Blake. Everyone was quiet for a minute engaged in their own thoughts before Blake interrupted the silence.

"I moved the rest of my stuff over grandma's last night". Blake stated.

"Blake you are the only person I know that would move your shit in the middle of winter's night". Said Ariel.

"I do what I have to do, besides Jay is trying to act stupid! He had the nerve to tell me if I was leaving that I had to have my shit out by today. I told his ass (no problem)". She said.

"No he ain't acting like that." Sydni exclaimed. "Yes he is". Said Blake.

Ariel got up and grabbed her purse. "I have to go. I'm meeting Lance for lunch at Bennigan's".

"So what's his story"? Mya asked.

"He is just cool as hell. I have never met anyone who could keep me laughing as much as he does. I let Isis meet him yesterday and she loves him. That's all she has been talking about". Said Ariel.

"So no girlfriend, I assume". Said Mya.

"Not that I know of. I'll talk to y'all later". She replied as she left them.

"So what do you think". Mya asked Blake.

"It's been my experience that if something seems too good to be true, then it usually is. What do you think Sydni"?

"Well my New Year's Resolution was not to criticize anyone before I examine my own backyard. So, I am gonna stay out of this one. Let's not spoil it for her".

Second Time ... Shame On Me.

CHAPTER 10

"Mya what the hell are you doing with a passion mark on your face"? Sydni asked.

"Girl, Jermaine is stupid. I told him he is so immature". Mya said. She knew they would die if they knew that he actually bit her. He was upset because some of her old friends were still calling her cell phone. So he smacked her once and bit her face. Mya was too embarrassed to admit that she was going through the same thing again. She promised herself that she was gonna leave Jermaine alone. It was just easier said than done, because he didn't want to leave.

After everybody ate, Sydni sat around for a minute and then went to pick up Eric. He had been staying with his grandmother. Eric was ecstatic when he saw his mommy she was equally excited to see him. She talked to his grandmother for a minute but Eric was anxious to leave, so she got him together thanked his grandmother, and left. Mrs. Fordson always liked Sydni and thought it was a shame that her grandson had let her get away.

Later on that evening after she had put Eric to bed, Sydni turned out all the lights and soaked up the darkness. She thought about her newfound relationship and asked herself was she happy? Deep in her heart she knew that she was still letting the past hurt her. She was happy to be involved again because she was losing at the dating game. But she wasn't 100% sure that Trevor was the right man for her. "Stop worrying so much". She told herself. "You always over analyze things. Just go with the flow." She finally drifted off to sleep a little after midnight.

Sydni had a lot on her mind, so much so that she forgot to give Ariel some money to deposit into her account. The first thing that she did when she woke up was to call Ariel.

"Hey, I meant to give you some money to deposit into my account yesterday. What time are you leaving for work?"

"I'm not." Ariel said.

"What's wrong with you"? Sydni asked.

"I just don't feel like it". She said.

"Did I catch you at a bad time? You sound pissed off". Sydni replied.

"I'm just mad because Lance was supposed to come over last night and he never showed up. I paged him all night and he never even called back. So now this morning he calls me from work and says that they asked him to come in last night to do a double".

"Okay, so what's wrong with that". Sydni asked.

"Nothing, but he could have at least called me and said something". Said Ariel

"Yeah, I guess that is true. I hate it when Trevor does that. What's so hard about calling"? Said Sydni.

"I honestly think they do that because they don't want to feel controlled. But let us try the same thing and all hell breaks loose". Said Ariel.

"I feel you. So since you aren't going to work, why don't you come down here and work out with me over at the spa"? Asked Sydni.

"Bet. I'll be there in twenty minutes".

Sydni and Eric had slipped on their gray jogging suits and were stretching when Ariel buzzed the door.

"We're on our way down." She said. She grabbed their work out bag and locked the door. When they got outside, Sydni asked her why didn't she bring Isis"? She told her that her mother wanted to keep her.

"And you know I didn't have a problem with that". Said Ariel

"Girl, I thank God everyday for my mother and sisters. If I didn't have them to watch Eric I would be stuck in the house all the time". Said Sydni.

"Yes we are definitely blessed". Said Ariel.

When they got to the gym, there was a nice crowd already assembled. Sydni recognized a few of her neighbors and waved. She and Ariel stretched some more and then started on the stair steppers. After ten minutes Ariel stepped off of the machine.

"Sydni, I don't how you do this shit. It hurts too bad".

"Ariel, get back on the damn thing! It's only been ten minutes. Eric can do longer than that". Sydni said.

"I'm finished". Ariel said as she laid back against the mirror with her towel wrapped around her neck.

"Look at you, all laid out like you've done something". Sydni said.

"Whatever". Said Ariel.

Ariel was ready to call it quits, but Sydni wouldn't have any part of that. So she coaxed her into going to the weight lifting room. It was jammed packed with muscular men, all willing to help "guide" the two women. The two girls gladly accepted their help. Eric even got into it he was lifting two pound dumbbells with both hands.

The girls lifted until Ariel punked out again. Then they went for a swim in the heated indoor Olympic size pool. After their swim they relaxed in the whirlpool.

"I needed this, I swear I did". Said Ariel.

"Well you know you are always welcome to come down here". Sydni said.

The two showered back at the apartment, and then decided to go to lunch in Royal Oak. This was a little suburb that shared the border. It was inhabited mostly by students and the younger generation. Its main street was home to many clothing and music shops. After lunch they strolled down Main Street. Mainly window-shopping. At the end of the block there was this little shop that didn't have a name on it. Sydni, always the curious one wanted to go in. When they opened the door the bells overhead rang. They looked around the shop for something of interest. It was very dark and empty. It didn't look like anything was for sale. Sydni noticed a table with tarot cards and a crystal ball on it. Ariel said "it's obvious no one is here so let's go."

"The door was unlocked so someone is here. Hello, is anybody here"? She called.

At first there was no answer, then they heard someone say. "Just a minute". Then from a curtained door a very petite woman appeared. She appeared to be White but Sydni could tell from her accent that she was Hispanic. She had her hair dyed blond but her eyebrows were brown. The woman asked them if they were interested in getting their cards read.

Sydni was definitely game, Ariel on the other hand wasn't as convinced as Sydni. The woman invited the girls to come in the back. Sydni pushed Ariel and they followed her to the back. This room looked a lot different from the front room. It was very bright and decorated in yellows and light blue. There was a couch in the waiting area of the room and a small table covered with a white tablecloth. On it lay another set of tarot cards. The woman introduced herself as "Maria".

Maria invited Ariel to sit down first. Sydni looked around. It was a very relaxing setting. She played with Eric while Ariel received her reading. Sydni couldn't hear what they were saying but after about ten minutes Ariel got up and came and sat down with Eric without saying a word to Sydni. She had a perplexed look on her face so Sydni didn't question her. She got up and went and sat at the table.

Sydni didn't know what to expect, and after seeing the look on Ariel's face she was a little apprehensive, but she was gonna go through with it. Maria immediately informed her that her readings usually only lasted no more than fifteen minutes, but she was going to need a little more time with her.

"That's scary". Sydni said.

"It's not that, I'm just picking up very strong vibes from you". Said Maria.

"First you must open yourself up to the reading." Said Maria. "Relax your mind and let all your worries rest for

173

now. Repeat after me. I welcome a message of wisdom and open myself to receive the guidance that I most need at this time."

Sydni did as she was told. Maria shuffled the cards and turned the top one over, it was the High Priestess.

"This card tells me that you are surrounded by people that need you. Not necessarily needy people but they love and admire you. It also tells me that you are a good friend. You can be trusted". Said Maria.

Sydni just listened she didn't want to give her any information that would help Maria give her a false reading.

"The next card is, the lovers. You are involved with someone right now. He is different from any man that you have ever dealt with. He offers you many challenges. You often find yourself compromising your beliefs or how you feel for him. Though I must say this man loves you. I don't

think there will ever be another man who will love you more. He is one of those people we spoke about that needs you. You bring stability to his unstable life. Because of this, his love is wicked and selfish. He will be very jealous and possessive of you. I would even go so far to say that one-day he may strike you. This will all be done in the name of his love for you."

Sydni was shocked. She could feel her body trembling

"I also sense the presence of another woman. He may not be involved with her sexually, but there is another woman around him. She does not want happiness between the two of you and you should watch for this woman to appear soon. Remember this does not have to mean a lover. This could be a relative, a friend or an ex-girlfriend. But don't be quick to judge, because you young lady are always surrounded by other men".

Sydni was sitting there like a sponge, soaking every word in. She was captivated by the accuracy of facts about her personality and that of Trevor.

"The next card is the Queen of Pentacle. The queen is the ultimate nurturing mother. The little boy out there is yours. "Obviously Sydni thought. He looks just like me."

"Yes, he is". Sydni said with a smile.

"He will never betray you. He is a small soldier willing to go to war for you. He sees you in a different light from everyone else. To him, you can do no wrong. Is he a vegetarian? Maria asked.

"No, but he only eats chicken and I have to force him". Answered Sydni.

"He needs to eat more, he's too thin".

"Is that what the cards say"? Sydni asked.

"No, just from my observation". Maria smiled.

Sydni looked over to Ariel who looked like she was ready to leave, so she asked Maria to read one more card then she would have to leave.

"The final card is the three of Pentacles. This card focuses on the group. As the Pentacles are grounded and practical, this card represents a task-oriented team-people that are working cooperatively toward a common goal. Sydni you must know that there are few jobs that can be accomplished alone. We need the help of others to achieve our goals. You will be more productive if you let people help you. You need to realize that you don't have to do it all by yourself. You always insist on carrying the burden alone, you don't have to. You are surrounded by helping and caring individuals, who will help you in times of need. Also, you have to let others learn their own lessons. Sometimes people stumble a few times before they walk the straight and narrow. Just be there to break their fall. Sydni you are a most intriguing subject. I would love to read for you again when you get a chance". Maria replied.

"Thank you Maria, you have given me some very good advice". Said Sydni as she stood up to leave. She shook Maria's hand but Maria didn't let go.

"Sydni remember the warnings I have given you. Do not ignore them.".

"I won't. Thanks again." She said as Maria let go of her hand.

After they left the shop neither Sydni or Ariel discussed their readings. They didn't have much to say during the ride home. They were both thinking about the little Hispanic lady, with the bleached blonde hair and brown eyebrows. As Sydni and Eric were getting out of her car, Ariel said.

"Sydni, you know that is just for entertainment purposes only. You are only supposed to take it at face value. So don't go getting all crazy about anything that she said. If it comes true, it's only coincidence".

"I know. I'll call you later". Said Sydni.

Sydni tried to reach Trevor on his cell phone when she got back home. He didn't answer. She and Eric watched TV until it was time for her to go to work. She dropped him off over Mama's so Rimy could watch him. By the time that she got back in the car her cell phone was ringing.

"Hello". Sydni answered.

"Hey, I saw that you called me". Said Trevor.

"Yeah I did. Where were you"? She asked.

"I was taking care of something.". Said Trevor.

"Really". Said Sydni. – "Yeah really. What's up with this line of questioning"? He asked.

"Nothing, I can't ask you where you've been"? Asked Sydni.

"Look I haven't even seen you all day. So I know whatever it is that has you pissy, has nothing to do with me. So call me when you get home". Said Trevor.

Sydni just hung up the phone. "I'm going crazy. That boy hasn't done anything to me. Let me stop tripping". She verbalized. She called his cell phone back but he didn't answer. "See that's the shit I'm talking about". She said as she hung up on his voicemail.

When she got to work she told Blake the edited version of her reading. She figured nobody needed to know the things that Maria had said about Trevor. Blake was mad because they hadn't called her.

"I can't believe you worked out without me and went to a psychic". Said Blake.

"I'm sorry. I will probably go back soon. Then we can go together". Said Sydni.

"Yeah, yeah." Blake replied. –

That night Trevor came over after Eric had gone to sleep. Sydni apologized for her behavior earlier and he accepted. After making love they laid in each other's arms. She knew he was asleep as she listened to his steady, even breathing. She loved the way he held her all night. Ever since that day at the bar he had been the ideal boyfriend. She knew she was in love with him, she was just too afraid to admit it. She hadn't loved anyone since Big Eric. She rolled over to face him, kissed his cheek and then his lips. He opened his eyes and smiled at her and kissed her back. "He won't hurt me". She told herself.

That morning she woke up when she felt someone standing over her. It was Eric and he didn't look happy. "Mama" he whispered. "Who is this man in your bed"?

"Oh my God." Sydni jumped up. She had completely forgot to lock her door. So much for trying to break him into the idea, she thought. Trevor had heard him by then.

"Hey man my name is Trevor. What is yours"? Said Trevor. – Eric looked at him and completely ignored him.

"Eric mind your manners boy. Don't you hear him talking to you". Said Sydni

"Mama you told me not to talk to strangers". Eric said. – "You are right sweetie. I sure did. This is Trevor, Eric. He is my new friend and he wants to be your friend too". Said Sydni. "Do you think that's possible?" Asked Trevor.

"I'll think about it". Eric said as he walked back into his room. Sydni fell back onto her pillow. She buried her face into her hands. "Oh shit, that didn't go well". She said.

"It'll probably take some time but he'll get used to me." Trevor said. "I hope so". Said Sydni.

After breakfast Sydni decided she wanted to do something special for Trevor's 30th birthday. She called up a travel agent she had used in the past and booked a trip to Jamaica. She only had two months so she needed to get some extra money being generated from somewhere. She thought.

They were supposed to meet Ariel and Lance for dinner that night, but Ariel cancelled because she hadn't heard from him. They ended up getting carry out because Trevor had a run he needed to make. She had been meaning to inquire about all these runs he had to make but decided against it. "What I don't know won't hurt me". She said.

Finally the snow was beginning to melt. The temperature was ranging in the fifties but that was better than the twenties. It had been a long winter for Sydni. She and Trevor were getting along well. They had learned a lot about each other. Some things they liked, others they didn't. Sydni was happy that Eric had finally loosened up a little with Trevor. Trevor had finally given up his apartment and moved in with them. Trevor paid the rent and car notes and Sydni was responsible for the groceries, utilities, the phone and her car insurance. So far everything was working out fine.

Sydni started working at the bar on Thursdays to pay for the trip. They had Karaoke on Thursdays at the bar. That night she and Mya were sitting at the bar talking. Mya was complaining about how Jermaine treated his daughter like she was a princess. "I keep telling him that no one gets special treatment in my house. All kids are treated the same. He thinks that every thing that she does is cute. But if Darius does something then he wants me to beat his ass." Said Mya.

"So the little girl's Mama doesn't mind you spending time with her daughter"? Sydni asked. –

"You know she does. Girl we went to the girl's birthday party and I had to put that bitch in check. She was walking

around showing off for her friends at first. Then I had to let her ass know, I ain't the one"! - "Don't tell me she tried to go there on you.". Sydni said.

"Yes, she did. But you know I handled my business. So now she doesn't say too much of anything, frankly I think she doesn't care because she has a babysitter now. So she is free to roam the streets with her ugly ass". Said Mya.

"Where is your car"? Asked Mya. – Trevor dropped me off today. I'm tired of driving that damn car, we are supposed to go look at new cars tomorrow". Said Sydni.

"Alright lets go finish working because Tony is going crazy over there. He was standing on the other side of the bar with both hands on his hips mouthing, "Am I the only one working tonight"? They laughed and started washing the glasses and ashtrays. Later that evening she wrote a check for the final payment on their trip.

Sydni knew exactly what kind of vehicle she wanted and she couldn't understand why Trevor was making the process harder than it really was. He had to read all the literature, try to talk the salesman down and do his own inspection of the car. Sydni figured the price was on the truck and that's what you were supposed to pay. She had her eyes on a candy apple red Lincoln Navigator. Their salesman was trying to convince Trevor that his price was the best that he was going to get. Trevor managed to talk him down $2000 and got him to upgrade the stereo system. Sydni's mouth dropped when the guy told her that they would need $5000 down payment to keep her car note where they wanted it. Trevor with no hesitation handed over 50 crisp $100 bills. She was surprised, she knew Trevor was generous, but he had never been that generous! She was on cloud nine when she drove out in her brand new truck.

Weekends at the bar were so profitable that Sydni hated she wasn't going to be there the following weekend. She was trying to get all the tips she could for her trip. She didn't want Trevor to have to spend any more money. This was her treat!

Ariel was looking gloomy. Sydni asked her what was wrong. – "Lately things have changed between me and Lance. He is so hard to keep up with now. He is always selling me out and standing me up. I paged him before I got here and he still hasn't called me back". She said.

"Well Ariel, it might be time to consider the fact that there might be someone else involved in his life." She said.

"I don't know but he sure has changed. You remember how we were". Said Ariel. – "Yeah, inseparable and sickening"! Sydni replied. As they were talking Melanie's boyfriend Everett walked up and commented.

"Hey Ariel, sorry about what happened". - "What are you talking about Everett"? Ariel asked.

"That's just messed up that Lance would go and get married, while y'all were suppose to be kicking it". Said Everett.

"What"! The girls said in unison. "What was that Everett?" Asked Sydni. "Aww man, don't tell me you didn't know". He said. "He left for Las Vegas this morning. He didn't even invite any of his boys". The pain in Ariel's eyes made Sydni cringe. Ariel ran to the bathroom.

Across the room Blake and Mya both saw her run into the bathroom so they followed her. When Sydni got there, Ariel was locked in a stall crying and Mya and Blake were trying to coax her out. "Fuck him". Said Blake. "He wasn't good enough for you anyway".

"That's alright Ariel. You know his ass has got to pay for this." Said Mya. "Ariel, I asked Everett did he know who the girl is, and he said yes. I think she should know that up until the day before her wedding her husband was intimately involved with someone". Said Sydni.

"Just forget it". Ariel cried. "Please y'all I just want to be left alone." Just then Tony busted in the door. "I know four ladies that are gonna be looking for jobs tomorrow if I don't get some waitresses on the floor and a barmaid behind the bar.

"Okay Tony, we just had an emergency". Said Mya. - "Y'all always have some kind of emergency going on. I don't want to hear it". He said. – They all rolled their eyes at him as they walked by.

"Keep on rolling em, but you better control em' if you want a job". "Damn girls. I swear they always got some drama, if they ain't fighting, they crying. I swear I can't take it no more". Tony said to himself.

When Ariel came out the girls already had the plan in motion. Come Monday, Lance was going to wish he was never born, nonetheless married.

The rest of the week was devoted to devising her plan and getting ready for her trip. She called her old boss Kris and asked for a huge favor. "You owe me". She said. "I told you to come back." Kris said. – "And deal with Marc and that old bat?" I don't think so. Just help me with this and we will be even". Said Sydni. "Remind me not to ever make you or any of your friends angry". Said Kris.

That Monday as Lance and his new wife drove home down interstate 94, they couldn't help but notice the newest billboard. It was a picture of Lance, an equal sign and a picture of a German shepherd. It read: Ladies beware! Don't get bit by this dog! Mrs. Shepherd the night before your wedding he ate a cat! Lance almost ran off the road!

The sun was shining so brightly Sydni could hardly see as she drove the long stretch up I-75. She put on her Gucci sunglasses and pulled down the sun visor. She was doing some last minute shopping for the trip. She had to pick up some swimming trunks for Trevor. He had agreed to meet at Somerset Mall at noon. She was running late as usual. When she pulled up in valet Trevor was just getting out of his car. He was on the phone so she reached up and kissed him. She got both valet tickets from the attendant and walked into Hudson's. He was walking behind her still on the phone. As she walked she passed two guys who tried to get her attention. She informed them that her man was walking behind and the moved on. One called back. "Let him know he is a lucky man." Trevor answered. "I know". As he got off the phone.

The guys kept walking. When he caught up with Sydni he was pissed. "That's the shit I'm talking about. Brothas love to disrespect one another".

"Trevor I don't think they were being disrespectful. I don't think they knew that I was with you". She said.

"So why are you sticking up for them? All you had to do was keep walking." He said. —"look bay, it's not that big of a deal. I don't want to argue, we have too much to do." She said as she reached up to kiss him.

They shopped around for some last minute items that they had to get. Sydni ended up buying Eric some more clothes and a new game boy cartridge that he wanted. She knew she was spoiling him but he was such a good kid.

That Thursday Paige dropped them off at the airport. Sydni laughed when she saw the billboard. Even though they had leased the board for a month, she knew Lance would be feeling the affects from that much longer. When they reached their terminal, Sydni reminded Paige to pick up Eric from the day care before 5Pm everyday, and to be careful in her truck.

Once they had boarded the plane Sydni willed herself to relax. She hated flying and it was Trevor's first time on a plane so they both were pretty nervous. Once they were in the air it was smooth sailing. It took 31/2 hours to get to Montego bay where they boarded a bus to Negril. The bus ride was crazy! There were no traffic signals or stop signs, so the drivers basically played chicken on the road. It was unnerving for the both of them. By the time they reached their hotel they had headaches and wanted to lie down. That all changed when they entered the courtyard of the hotel and saw the Negril Gardens. It was beautiful with tropical flowers growing everywhere. Sydni was overwhelmed by it's beauty. That was all cut short when she saw a lizard run past her sandal. She almost jumped on Trevor's back. The bellhop told her that they were harmless and more afraid of her than she was of them.

Their room was as beautiful as the courtyard. It was very spacious and clean. There was a window overlooking the courtyard much to Sydni's delight. Trevor tipped the bellhop and started to undress. "I have to take a shower. It is hot as hell." He said. While Trevor was showering Sydni slipped in with him. A fifteen-minute shower turned into thirty.

Later after they showered Sydni slipped on a sundress and Trevor put on some Nautica shorts and a matching T-Shirt. They both left their shoes and walked down to the beach. The hotel had an outdoor bar that sat on the beach. They ordered drinks and walked down the beach. It was noon and already 89 degrees. But there was a breeze coming off the ocean that made the heat bearable. People were swimming and Jet Skiing. Trevor couldn't wait to try that! He seemed genuinely happy to be there. She was surprised to learn that he had never been anywhere outside of the neighboring state of Ohio.

They went back to their room and changed into their swimsuits. It cost them $35 in American money to rent the jet skies for thirty minutes. They had a ball, though neither of them could swim. When they turned them back in Trevor said. "This could be really fun if Justin and the crew had come." Sydni couldn't believe her ears! All the money and time it took her to plan a romantic trip for him and he tells her it would be better if a group of guys had come with them. Her feelings were really hurt.

"You know, if that's the way you feel then maybe you should have had your boys bring you to Jamaica. I can't believe that you are even thinking about them while you are here with me".

"What? All I said was that it would be fun if they were here." Said Trevor. It was obvious that he couldn't understand why she was feeling the way that she was.

"Trevor, I'll be glad when you decide to grow up. I hope one day soon your idea of a fun evening will change from hanging around a bunch of brothas to being with that special someone." Said Sydni. With that she stalked down the beach. Trevor just stood there looking confused.

Sydni walked the beaches thinking about what had just happened. She went into one of the huts stationed on the beach. Sydni was immediately overwhelmed by marijuana smoke. Once she could see through the smoke she saw who she assumed was the shop owner. He welcomed her to his hut and resumed smoking his pipe. She looked around for a minute at the statues and vases then got the creeps when she noticed him staring at her. It didn't help that when she stalked away from Trevor she had forgotten to get her cover-up, so she was walking the beach in a skimpy bikini. She also didn't have any money on her so she excused herself and told him that she would be back later. He said. "Make sure you do".

She hurried up and got out of there. Sydni was a little buzzed from the smoke, so the fresh air did her some good. She went back to the beachside bar at the hotel and ordered a drink. Trevor was nowhere in sight and she was happy about it. She charged the drink to her room. "He is rude as hell and not to mention ungrateful. I bust my ass to bring him on this trip and he would rather be with his boys". Sydni thought to herself. She sat and watched a group of little kids swimming with their mom. She thought about Eric and wished now that she had brought him. "At least he would appreciate it". She thought.

Second Time ... Shame On Me.

CHAPTER 11

They had reservations to take a "Glass Bottom Cruise" at 5 o'clock So Sydni went back to the room to change. When she walked into the room there was a beautiful bouquet of tropical flowers on the vanity. There was also a gorgeous sundress laid out on the bed with a card. She opened the card and all it said was "I'm sorry". She had almost started to cry when Trevor walked into the room. She started to say something but he interrupted her.

"Wait Sydni, let me say something first. I'm really sorry that I hurt your feelings earlier. I didn't realize what I had said until it was too late. You have to realize that I have never had a girlfriend before and I don't know what to say or do to make you feel special like you should. I have never had to make someone happy and I'm just learning with you. You mean everything to me and I need you in my life. You make me so happy and I'm going to work on making you happy too".

Sydni was speechless. This was the first time he had ever opened up to her like this. She got up and hugged him. She thanked him for the flowers and the dress. They changed and got ready for the cruise.

Once they boarded the boat it was literally "smooth sailing". Because the boat had a glass bottom they could see the fish and the reefs under the boat. It was beautiful. Sydni took pictures of the falls and the mountains. Their host served them a chicken dish that was served with rice. It was delicious. They drank Jamaican rum and danced to reggae music. It was so much fun. The sun began to set, that was a sight to see. It seemed like the sun was sinking into the ocean. Sydni had never seen anything like it. She was happy to be sharing this evening with Trevor. She watched him as he took pictures of the sunset and fell deeper in love with him.

By the time that they got back to the room they were exhausted. It had been a long day. Sydni called to check on Eric and her truck. She was happy to hear that both were okay. She talked to Eric for a minute and then retired for the evening.

The next day they went horseback riding in the hills and Sydni was appalled to see how the town people lived. Their homes were shacks. They looked like they would fall down if a gust of wind blew through the town. Trevor acknowledged that they were "truly blessed".

The next few days went by in a flash. They were leaving Sunday morning, which was Trevor's actual birthday. Saturday night she surprised him at dinner. She had their waitress bring out a birthday cake and everyone joined her in singing "happy birthday" to him. He was embarrassed but he was really happy.

"This is definitely the best birthday I've ever had". He said.

They had a safe trip back home and were happy when the plane touched down. Later that day they distributed all of the gifts that they had bought. Sydni showed off her suntan and told all of her friends about the trip. Trevor called his mom to let her know that he was back and she informed him that his grandfather had passed away. They had made arrangements for his funeral to be held that Thursday. He was devastated when he hung the phone up. Sydni knew that something terrible had happened. Trevor sat on the couch and put his head in his hands.

"Baby what's wrong"? She asked. Trevor looked at her with tears in his eyes and told her that his grandfather had passed. Sydni sat down next to him and held him as he cried softly. This was the first time Sydni had ever seen Trevor cry and it hurt her deeply. She wiped away her own tears as she told him that it would be okay, and that they would make it through this together.

The days before the funeral were hard for Trevor. He wasn't accepting any calls and he didn't go anywhere. The day of the funeral he wanted Sydni to ride in the family car with him. She held his hand when they viewed the body, and sat with him through the service. It was heartbreaking to see him going through that much pain. Somehow they made it through the day, together.

It had been over a week since they had been back and she wished that they were still in Jamaica. She missed the sunshine and the beach. The weather in the city was awful. It was another rainy day as Sydni drove to work. It was so depressing. Blake had acquired a voicemail box from some radio station and was listening to all these strange lonely men that had left messages.

"Blake you cannot be serious about this". Said Sydni.

"There is nothing wrong with this Sydni, not everyone wants to go to the bar to meet someone". Said Blake. – "Yeah, but aren't you afraid you might hook up with some serial killer or something"? Asked Sydni.

"I haven't hooked up with anyone yet. I'm just listening to what they have to say right now". Said Blake. – "Alright, whatever works, just let me know when you decide to go out with someone so we will know where your ass is". Sydni said.

"You know I will". Said Blake.

Sydni was excited as hell, the lottery had just come out and she had hit it! The first thing that came across her mind was that she could replace some of the money she had spent on that trip.

Trevor called her cell phone and asked her to come pick him up from the bar. He had rode there with someone else and he was ready to leave. When he got in the truck he pulled out a picture. The picture was of a beautiful baby girl. "Oh she's cute. Whose baby is this"? Sydni asked.

"Mine". Trevor said. The baby couldn't have been anymore than five months. Sydni quickly did the math.

"What the hell do you mean yours? Trevor you didn't tell me you had someone pregnant." She screamed.

"I know I was going to, but I kept forgetting.". Said Trevor as he shrugged his shoulders.

"Forgetting? How do you forget that you have a baby on the way? I can't believe you kept this from me all this time, then out of the fucking blue you decide to drop this bomb on me!" Sydni was devastated and it was clearly evident by the look on her face.

"What's the big deal? This happened before you and I were together". Said Trevor

"Okay, but you should have told me. You should have given me the chance to decide whether or not I wanted to deal with this". She said.

"What do you mean deal with this? Me and Sherry have been broke up for a long ass time". Said Trevor

A silent bell rang in Sydni's head as she drifted back to the day when she received the phone call from the unidentified caller who asked to speak to Sherry. She had clearly caught him in a bold lie. "Who did you say"? She asked.

"I said Sherry, my baby mama". He said.

Sydni pulled the truck over to the side of the road. "Get the hell out"! She said as she unlocked the doors.

"What? It's raining like hell out there. I ain't getting out." He said defiantly.

"Get out Trevor because you are a liar and I don't want to deal with this shit".

"What did I lie about"? Asked a stupefied Trevor.

"You know what it doesn't even matter. But you think about it, maybe it'll come to you. I just know I can't trust your ass. You've hid your child from me for all these months and a relationship that I knew nothing about, and you don't think there is anything wrong with that"? Asked Sydni.

"Leave it to you, I can't do shit right. I call myself being honest and telling you about the baby but just because I didn't do it when Sydni wanted me to do it, I'm wrong". Said Trevor as he locked the doors back.

"No Trevor you are wrong because you didn't give me the opportunity to decide if this was something that I wanted to accept. Besides you hid your own flesh and blood from me". Sydni said as she unlocked the doors again.

"Well I didn't have a problem accepting Eric"! Said Trevor.

"Year, but I didn't hide the fact that I had a child. You knew from the beginning so you could have walked away then." Said Sydni.

"Is that what you want Syd? You want to walk away? Well, it ain't happening. You think you are going to come in my life and change things around then walk away? My baby is here now and we can't change that. So just deal with it." He laid back in his seat and locked the door again.

Sydni was shocked. She couldn't muster enough energy to curse him out, instead she sat back in her seat and drove home.

That night as she lay in bed, she thought to herself. "I know I should be putting his ass out right now. What is holding me back? He was so wrong and I'm just supposed to get over it. How can I trust him after he hid something so important from me."? It was like Trevor was reading her mind because he kissed her shoulder and turned her over.

"Baby I'm sorry. I should have told you but I was afraid that I would lose you."

"Trevor withholding something from me is as bad as lying. I can deal with a bad truth better than dealing with a lie".

"I guess I just thought that you wouldn't want to fuck with me anymore because of the whole Sherry thing".

"Well my first question is are you and Sherry involved in any other capacity, other than parents to your little girl? By the way what is her name"?

"Her name is Nia, and no me and Sherry broke up when she was pregnant and I don't mess with her like that". Trevor said in his most convincing voice.

"So I don't have to worry about her tripping right? Because you know I am not for any bullshit. I know it is possible to maintain a responsible relationship between a child's mutual parents without it being any shit in the game. I do it everyday". Sydni said, making her position very clear.

"You don't have to worry about that. I just hate that my grandfather never got a chance to meet her". He said.

"I'm sorry too baby." Sydni said as she kissed his cheek. They cuddled until they both fell asleep.

Sydni's emotions had ran the gamut all the way from the lowest point to a high point as she dealt with her new found knowledge. The one thing that she knew for sure was that she loved Trevor, and she believed with her heart that Trevor loved her. What she wanted most was a reasonable explanation that she could live with.

The next day she had made plans to hook up with Blake.

"So what's happening today"? Sydni asked.

"I'm going out with my new friend Terry. The guy I've been talking to from the dating hotline". Blake replied.

Just then Trevor walked into the kitchen. "Who are you talking to?" He asked as he opened the fridge and pulled the orange juice out. He was about to drink out of the carton, but Sydni grabbed it first and answered. "Blake....okay so where are ya'll going"? She asked Blake as she reached for a glass and poured him some juice.

"We're going to meet for drinks at Montanas in Westland at nine".

"So you will be calling me at ten right"? Sydni asked.

"You aren't talking to no Blake! Who is that"? Asked Trevor.

"I said Blake, Trevor. Why do I need to lie?" Asked Sydni. He finished his juice and walked out of the kitchen".

"Anyway girl, you sure you don't want us to go with you on this first date"? Sydni asked.

"Girl, you are not going to get on my nerves! Terry is a nice guy and we are only meeting for drinks, not going to the hotel". Laughed Blake.

"You don't know him from Adam". Sydni mumbled.

"Oh stop worrying so damn much Sydni. Live a little girl. I'll see you at work". Blake stated as they hung up.

"Why are you questioning me about who I'm talking to Trevor"? She asked as he walked into the bedroom.

"Because I can". He said and walked out of the bedroom and threw his coat on to leave. "I love you". He called up the stairs.

"Whatever". Sydni mumbled as she ran her bath water. She called Ariel and set up her own little date!

Blake got to Montana's fifteen minutes early. She had to make sure she was looking her best. She had brought her clothes to work so she would be on time. She took one final

196

look at herself and said. "This is it". Blake took a seat at the bar where they had agreed to meet. She had just ordered a glass of wine when a gorgeous guy walked through the door. "Oh my God. Please be him." She thought to herself. She was disappointed when she saw him walk over to a table where another guy was sitting. She was even more disappointed when she saw him bend down and kiss him. "I swear all the good men are either married or gay". She said to herself. Just then an equally gorgeous guy tapped Blake on the shoulder.

"Blake"? "There is a God". Blake thought.

Blake and Terry were deeply engrossed in a conversation when Sydni and Ariel slipped in. It had cost Sydni twenty dollars to get the table she needed. It was a discreet table but she still had a bird's eye view of Blake at the bar.

"Girl, he is fine". Ariel stated.

"You don't have to be ugly to be a serial killer". Said Sydni. "You are crazy, but you know Blake is going to kill us if she finds out we are here.". Ariel replied.

"Well, this is for her own good. She is too damn trusting". Sydni replied as she peered over the top of her menu.

"Yeah, something you need to try to be more of......Jamesetta Bond". Ariel stated as she rolled her eyes at her friend.

"Whatever, ya'll won't be saying that shit if something happens to her". Said Sydni.

"Knock on some wood, fool". Said Ariel. They both knocked on the table. "Well I'm about to order some crab legs since we are here. You know they have the bomb-ass seafood here." Said Ariel as she looked over the menu.

"No-o-o-o, what if they get up to leave"?

"Then they just leave. Sydni you really are crazy. You need to have your head examined. Got me all twisted in this 007 shit." Ariel stated as she signaled to the waiter that she was ready to order.

"Well, order me a shrimp cocktail, greedy ass". Said Sydni keeping her eye on Blake.

Blake was having the time of her life. Terry was all that she had expected and more. She had made it a point not to expect Denzel Washington but this man was fine. She couldn't believe that he was single and didn't have any children. He was a Detroit City Fireman and was on duty just eight days out of the month. He remodeled HUD houses in his spare time. She liked the fact that he was interested in her children and wanted to know more about her. Their conversation was going well until Terry asked her about her soon to be ex-husband. Even though she had filed for a divorce it still was a sore subject for her. She knew she could never help Jay unless he wanted to help himself but it still hurt to see someone you care about suffer. Terry picked up on the sadness and changed the subject.

"Do you know those two women sitting over there"? He asked. I noticed them staring and pointing in our direction".

Blake looked to where he was pointing but only saw two people with their menus raised unusually high. Blake was sure she didn't know them so they continued their conversation.

"Let's go Sydni! He almost ratted us out". Ariel replied. "Well she didn't see us so we are alright." Sydni said even though she had to admit that it was a close call.

"Look I'm about to go. Blake is a grown ass woman and is obviously having a beautiful time unlike myself, over here looking like a damn fool. I'm outta here". Ariel said.

"Sellout". Said Sydni. – "Shut up". Said Ariel. As she turned to walk away she bumped right into their waiter. His whole tray toppled to the floor. Suddenly everyone in the restaurant was looking their way, including Blake and Terry.

"Sydni and Ariel, what the hell are you two doing here"? Blake asked stressing her agitation in her voice. Sydni was helping the waiter up and wiping him off. He grabbed the napkin from her and wiped himself off.

"I'm just trying to help". She said as she walked over to where Ariel was ratting her out.

"It was all Sydni's idea. She thought you were hooking up with some mass murderer and so we should follow you to make sure you were okay". Ariel made her plea.

"So much for being in this together Ariel". Sydni said. Ariel shrunk back and started picking her nail.

"Syd, I told you I was okay. I really wish you wouldn't take it upon yourself to be our mother. I'm a big girl and I can handle myself". Blake said. She heard Terry clearing his throat. "Terry these are two of my best friends, Sydni and Ariel".

"It's my pleasure, I've heard so much about both of you". He said as he shook their hands.

"Please let me apologize Terry. I am so sorry for judging you. I guess I can be a little over protective of my friends sometimes". Said a blushing Sydni.

"A little? Sometimes? I think not." Said Ariel. Sydni threw her a dirty look.

"But that's why we love her so much." Said Blake as she gave Sydni a hug. From that Sydni knew she was forgiven.

"I'm sorry that I ruined your date". She said to Blake and Terry. "That's the least of your problems". Said Blake as she pointed to the waiter who was holding out a bill for the food and damages.

When Sydni got home she called Mama to share their experience at the restaurant. Ultimately she started to talk about Trevor and her problems with him. This was a regular subject that she talked about with Mama.

"Time and time again. He is always running the streets, but he trips if I go out and I'm just getting tired of it. I miss my freedom."

"Sydni before you jump the gun and leave him, because I know that is what you are thinking. Take a minute to go over everything and make sure everything is as bad as you say it is. If it is then you just might have to reconsider the situation but don't just give up. You have to remember we are all imperfect. His flaws might be able to be worked out. The next man might be worse!"

"I know Ma. I think I'm just talking crap. I just need to vent every now and then. Thanks for listening and the advice, Mama." Sydni said as she hugged her mom. As she was driving home she thought to herself that she was going to make this work even if it killed her.

She was still awake at 5 o'clock in the morning when Trevor slipped in the bed. She pretended to be sleep. "Right back, huh"? She thought as that is what he had told her before he left.

The next day when Sydni got home she called Mya she had not heard from her in several days. There was a recording saying that the number had been disconnected. That seemed a little strange, but shit happens, she thought. After she got dressed she went over to her house to assure herself that everything was alright. When she got there the house looked empty from the outside, no drapes were on the windows. She knocked on the door, but there was no answer. She called Ariel and Blake on her cell phone and asked had either of them talked to her. They both said no. Now Sydni was really getting scared. It was unlike Mya to disappear without calling. Sydni paged her and she never returned her calls. She would never have let her phone get disconnected she thought. Her first thought after surveying the situation was to call the Police and report her missing. "No, I'm gonna call her grandmother, she probably knows where Mya is." She thought.

It took Syndi two days before she finally caught up with Mya's grandmother. She had been out of town visiting a sick sister in Ohio.

"Mrs. Fletcher this is Sydni. How are you today?"

"I'm fine honey, how you doing?"

"I'm okay, but I called because I am worried about Mya. We hadn't talked for about three days, so I called her. The phone had been disconnected so I went by. Her house was vacant, I could tell because the drapes and curtains were gone. I rang the bell and knocked just to be sure, but there was no answer. It is not like Mya to just leave without talking to us. So, I am very worried about her. I called you to find out if you knew anything about her whereabouts.?"

"Baby, the last time that I talked to her was two weeks ago. She said that she was thinking about re-locating to another state. She didn't say where, but she did say that she would let me know when she made up her mind for sure. I haven't talked to her since then, other than to call and leave a message on her answering machine that I was going to Ohio to see my sister who was sick. I'm sure she's okay. But if I hear from her, I will get in touch with you. I got your phone number in my book". She said.

"Thank you so much Mrs. Fletcher, I feel a lot better now, even though I still don't know why Mya didn't call me before she left. Have a good day".

Sydni spent the rest of the day trying to figure out why Mya had acted in this manner. She wasn't mad at any of them as far as she knew. She called Blake and Ariel and told them of her conversation with Mrs. Fletcher.

Blake said. "I guess it's the 3 Musketeers now." Sydni said. "Yeah, I guess."

Since she had given Melanie back her Thursdays at the bar, Sydni decided to meet Ariel and Blake at the bar for drinks. They were worried about Mya's sudden disappearance. Mrs. Fletcher's comments about her talking about relocating helped some, but it didn't eliminate all of their concerns. They knew that Jermaine had strange ways. When they got to the bar Ariel went behind the bar to see if Saturday was Mya's scheduled day to work. Much to her dismay she saw that Mya's name had been scratched off the schedule.

Ariel stood frozen in thought for several seconds. She then took the schedule and showed it to Sydni and Blake. Blake went and asked Tony what was going on.

"I thought you three knew before me. Mya quit a few days ago." Said Tony.

"What." They said in unison. "Okay, seriously y'all. We have to do something." Said Sydni. " Mya had a sister but they had stopped speaking shortly after their parents were killed in a car accident. They had never really got along, so there is no point in calling her. Sydni thought out loud to the girls".

"Well y'all know how Mya can get sometimes. Maybe she got into one of her moods and just doesn't want to talk right now". Ariel said.

"She only got like that with you". Ariel and Mya were constantly at each other's throats. We'll wait it out for a few more days. I'm sure she will call one of us soon". Said Blake.

"Well it's kind of dead here, lets go to the Paradise". Ariel suggested. Sydni's first mind said "no" but her mouth said okay. She should have followed her mind.

The Paradise was off the hook, as usual. Sydni got them in free and they went to find a table. She knew Trevor was there but she didn't see him at first. When she did see him, some little hoochie was all in his face. She calmly walked up to him and said. "I just wanted to let you know I was here. So you can let all the hookers and hoes know to be on their best behavior".

Sydni looked the hoochie straight in the eye and turned around. Trevor called after her.

"Come here". He pushed past the girl and walked up to Sydni. "Yeah, well you better be on your best behavior. Don't let me see no brotha up in your face".

"Don't even go there". Said Sydni.

Blake and Ariel were already on the dance floor so Sydni sat down at the table. It wasn't long before a guy walked over to the table.

"I know you aren't here by yourself". He said.

"No, actually I'm here with two of my friends". Said Sydni.

"Do you mind if I sit down?" He asked. "Well, yes because my boyfriend is here and I don't think he would appreciate it". She said.

"Oh well, I definitely don't want to step on anybody's toes. But I enjoyed these thirty seconds that I've spent talking to you". He said as he walked away.

Sydni smiled and sipped her drink. What she didn't notice was Trevor on the other side of the bar staring at her. He walked over to her table and asked could he talk to her for a minute. She got up and they walked outside.

When Ariel and Blake came back to the table they noticed Sydni had drank half of her drink. "She must have gone to the bathroom." Said Blake. "I don't know but I'm about to finish her drink". Said Ariel.

Outside Trevor was grilling Sydni about the conversation that she'd had with the guy in the bar. "Trevor, it wasn't a conversation. I told him that he couldn't sit at our table and that was it". She said. Sydni could tell that he was already drunk so she didn't want to push him.

"I thought I told you that you were too friendly. You are always up in somebody's face". Slurred Trevor.

What are you talking about? I wasn't in his face and you got a lot of nerve. I walk in the bar and you have some bitch all in your face, but did I say anything?" Asked Sydni.

"You know I don't give a damn about these hoes". Said Trevor.

"Whatever." Said Sydni.—"Let's go home". Trevor said.

"Trevor I'm not ready to go home. Besides, I came with my friends". She said.

"Fuck your friends. That's all you care about is your friends. Do I mean anything to you? You come here and disrespect me in front of all my friends, but I'm supposed to give a damn about yours". He said.

"You don't know the first thing about respect Trevor. If I hadn't come here tonight, it's no telling what would've went down between you and that bitch". Said Sydni.

"You better watch your mouth Sydni". He said.

"Excuse me? I am a grown ass woman. I'm tired of your controlling ways Trevor." Said Sydni. As she turned to walk away, Trevor grabbed her arm.

205

"I'm not trying to control you. I'm just demanding that you show me some respect". He said.

"Let me go". She said as she snatched away from him.

"Man I swear you make me want to slap the shit out of you sometimes".

"So that's next! What? Are you gonna beat my ass next, Trevor"?

"Man quit tripping. If I was going to do that I would have done it a long time ago". Said Trevor.

It was obvious to Sydni that this argument was never going to end and the parking attendants were enjoying the show, so she decided to cut it short.

"Trevor I'm not going to argue with you anymore about this. Let's just go". Said Sydni. She walked back into the club.

Blake and Ariel could immediately tell that something was wrong when she walked up to the table. "What's wrong with you"? Ariel asked. "Nothing, I'm about to go". Said Sydni.

"Damn, we just got here and it is off the hook." Said Blake. "I know but he is tripping and we better go before it escalates into something bigger". She said.

"Well, okay, but call me later". Said Blake. "I will. Y'all have fun". Said Sydni.

On the way home Sydni didn't have anything to say to Trevor. It helped that he was so drunk that he fell right to sleep anyway.

When they got home Sydni called Mama. "I can't believe that I'm right back where I was with Mike. I hate being treated like a possession. I am my own woman. I don't belong to anyone. I hate that he is like that because I love him so much. The crazy thing about all of this is he doesn't do anything special to make me love him. It's just something about him that I can't resist". Said Sydni.

"Well Sydni, you know that comes with the territory. I've never judged anyone that you've gone out with because I felt you were responsible enough to choose the right kind of guy. But when a person is used to the streets and all that comes with that life, they tend to be a little hardcore. Even to the people that they love. What you have to do is decide if you can deal with that or not". Said Mama.

"I just don't know if I can deal with someone who doesn't know how to treat me. I mean granted, he could be doing worse things, but I just don't like him doing me like this". She said. "I always attract guys like this". Said Sydni.

"Well, look where you hang out at, the bars. What type of men do you expect to meet there? Go to some different places and maybe you might meet a different kind of a man." Said Mama. "In the mean time, what are you going to do about Trevor"? Mama asked.

"I don't know Mama. I really don't know". Said Sydni

"Well if you love him like you say you do, don't rush into anything. Just take your time and think it over. It will all work out, I'm sure". Said Mama.

"Thanks Mama. I'll call you tomorrow." She said as she hung the phone up. She then went upstairs where Trevor was snoring away. "I'm good to his ass and I know that I deserve better. I'm tired of being embarrassed in public, harassed about who I'm talking to and where I've been. I'm just tired." She thought as she climbed in the bed.

The next morning Sydni still wasn't talking to Trevor. She went to work out and that helped her mood a little bit. She was walking on the stair stepper when she made eye contact with a gentleman on the other side of the room. They smiled at each other and looked away. "Damn, he is a nice looking White Boy." She thought. He was very tan and had jet- black hair. He had strong features and a body that wouldn't quit! She looked again and noticed he was still looking at her. She smiled again and laughed to herself. "What the hell are you doing"?

Lorenzo Lorenzetti was thinking the same thing. He had always been drawn to women of color, but he found himself really attracted to the young lady across the room. He walked over and introduced himself.

Sydni was shocked that he was so forward with her. "I want to apologize for staring but I'm captivated by your beauty". He said.

"Well thank you". Said as she looked at his well sculpted arms. There was definitely an immediate physical attraction between the two of them.

" I was wondering if I could interest you in a cup of coffee. There is a fabulous coffee shop in Greektown if you are interested".

"I would love to but I'm involved with someone and I wouldn't want him meeting someone for coffee. So I have to decline, this time".

"Well, what if I go get the coffee and bring it here? Technically you wouldn't be meeting me, because we are already here". Said Lorenzo. Sydni laughed.

"If that's the case then you don't have to go all the way to Greektown. They have a coffee machine downstairs".

They went downstairs and sat on one of the couches in the Lounge area of the Spa. Sydni learned that he was Italian. He had two older brothers and was a student at University of Detroit Law School. She gave him her background information. They had talked for an hour before Sydni's cell phone rang. She excused herself and answered it.

"Hello". "Where are you"? Trevor asked.

"I'm over at the Spa". Sydni said with an attitude.

"I know you aren't still tripping about last night, are you"? Trevor asked.

She looked over at Lorenzo and he flashed a perfect smile to her. "No, I'm not tripping". She told Trevor that she would be home shortly and hung up to continue her conversation with Lorenzo.

"So there is no way I can give you a call"? Lorenzo asked.

"As much as I would like to give you a number, I can't".

"I can appreciate you being loyal to your man. Maybe I'll come see you at the bar one day". He said.

"Yeah, you should. It was really nice talking to you. And good luck with your summer classes". Said Sydni as she grabbed her gym bag. Lorenzo took the bag instead and said.

"At least let me walk you to your car". She said okay.

Outside at the car, both Sydni and Lorenzo found it very hard to say good-bye. Finally after a few uncomfortable minutes of silence Sydni got into her car and drove off.

When she got home Trevor was getting out of the shower. "Damn, baby I have a headache. Can you get me some aspirin"? Sydni reached up into the medicine cabinet and thought to herself. "When are you going to serve me"? She gave him the pills and went to turn on the shower for herself.

"Are you working tonight"? Trevor asked.

"Don't I work every Friday"? She thought to herself but said. "Yes".

"Why don't you take off tonight, I'll pay you for the day. I think we need to spend some quality time. Don't you"? He asked. "Oh now you want to spend quality time". She thought but she said.

"Yeah, sure". After she showered she called Eric to see what he was doing over his dad's. He was playing on his Playstation and asked her to call him back.

"Well excuse me for interrupting". She told him. He said okay and hung up. Sydni was a little hurt at first but she decided to let it go. "He doesn't know what I'm going through". She thought.

Sydni and Trevor went to a Caribbean Restaurant on Larned called Jada for lunch. She picked over her food while Trevor tried to eat between phone calls on his cell phone. They then rode around for the better part of the day making his "runs". By the time they had figured out what they were going to do for the rest of the day, Sydni had a headache and was ready to go back home. He convinced her to go to a movie. It turned out to be a disaster because his phone rang throughout the whole movie. Sydni spent 90% of the movie watching it alone. When he did finally sit back down he asked her what had happened. It was impossible for her to tell him the whole movie, so she ignored him. He knew she had an attitude so he sat back and watched what was left of the movie.

On their way back home Trevor watched as Sydni stared out of the window. She hadn't said anything since they had left the theater.

"Do I make you unhappy"? He asked.

"What are you talking about"?

"You are sitting there like you lost your best friend. If something is wrong don't you think you should tell me"?

"Trevor, I think we need some time apart. I need to take some time to evaluate things". Sydni said.

"Evaluate What Man? I'm tired of having this same conversation Sydni. If you want me to leave I will, maybe I'm just not good enough for you. Go find you someone else who is willing to kiss your ass because I'm tired of doing it". He said.

"I don't want to argue with you. I just need some space. I feel smothered. I have a lot going on in my life that doesn't

211

even matter to you. Like one of my friends has basically dropped off the face of the earth and you have yet to ask me what is up with that? Things that are important to me don't mean anything to you. It's like my issues don't count. As long as you know where I am at all times, you really don't care what's going on in my life". Said Sydni.

"Have you ever considered the fact that Mya might not want to be found? Maybe she is happy wherever she is and she doesn't want to be bothered". Said Trevor.

"That isn't like Mya to do something like that. I don't want someone to kiss my ass Trevor. I want someone who is willing to treat me like I'm supposed to be treated. I don't deserve this shit that you are putting me through. You need to find you someone who doesn't give a damn about you and doesn't mind being dogged".

"Well, I'll get my shit and go as soon as we get back". Trevor said. "That's fine". Sydni replied.

Sydni sat in the living room and listened to him packing his clothes. She had that huge lump in her throat like she wanted to cry but she held it in. She fought the urge to run upstairs and tell him that she was sorry and she didn't want him to leave. When he was all packed he stopped at the bottom of the stairs. He turned to say something but the words caught in his throat. He shook his head and walked out. Sydni finally broke down and cried.

After a bit she turned off her ringer and went to bed. If this was what she really wanted, why did it hurt so bad? She tossed and turned all night. She finally couldn't help herself.
She dialed his cell phone number but he didn't answer. She threw the phone at the wall.

When morning came she dragged herself out of the bed, into the shower. She put on a old jogging suit and gym shoes. She went and got her hair done and a manicure. Sydni avoided any questions regarding her relationship with Trevor. After she was done she met Paige and Rimy for lunch.

When she pulled up Rimy started in on her. "What the hell is wrong with you? The Navi (her nickname for the truck) is not sparkling and you look like hell. You need to throw that jogging suit away. It is too tight on your butt".

"Leave me alone Rimy. I'm not in the mood". Sydni said.

"What happened now? Have y'all heard anything from Mya"? Paige asked.

"No, that's just one more thing that has me messed up. Me and Trevor broke up last night".

"Why"? Rimy asked.

"He was too sweet, with his ballin' shot callin' ass". Said Rimy. She looked at Rimy and just shook her head. Mama had said it before that Rimy was the spitting image of Sydni. Sydni hated that all the wrong things were attractive to her. She could see Rimy headed right in the same direction that she was. There was never a time that Rimy's hair was out of place. She didn't have bad days or days when she didn't feel like putting on her best clothes. You would never catch Rimy in the jogging suit that Sydni had on.

"Yeah, he was sweet but I don't want to talk about it anymore. What's up with y'all"? Sydni asked.

213

"Nothing, Mama has been tripping about my curfew. She wants me to be home by one o'clock". Rimy said.

"Be grateful for that. When I was your age I was a senior because of the way my birthday fell and I had the same curfew. At least you are only a junior. Imagine coming home from all the senior outings at one". Said Sydni "What's been up with you and Zo Paige"?

"I hate you brought up that name, he is smothering me Sydni. I can't go out with my friends without him tripping". Said Paige.

"Oh no! They are both mirror images of me". She thought. "Well Paige you have to demand that he give you space. You two are way too young to be tied down to each other. I'm not saying leave him but you need your friends. You know brothas come and go but your friends, your true friends will be there after he is gone". Enough of this depressing shit! Let's go shopping! I have to go see my baby first though. I haven't seen him in four days". Said Sydni.

Shopping always made Sydni feel better, but not this time. All she could think about was Trevor. She almost bought him a shirt that she knew he would like, but changed her mind.

Everyone was smiling when she walked in the bar that night to work. "Why is everyone looking like that"? She asked.

"Who was the Rico Suave that brought these flowers in last night"? Asked Melanie.

"Lanie, what are you talking about"? Sydni asked.

"A fine ass White Boy brought you this big ass bouquet of flowers and we all were hating your ass". She handed Sydni a card. "He left this. We started to open it but we knew you would be tripping". She said.

Sydni opened the card. It was a plain card, no picture or saying on the front. The inside simply read. "I can't stop thinking about you". It was signed L. Sydni smiled when she remembered her encounter from the day before.

"I can't believe he did this". She said.

"I can't believe you are kicking with a White Boy". Blake said.

"He is Italian". Sydni explained.

"Tomaytoe, tomahto, it's all the same to me". Said Blake.

"And I'm not kicking it with him. We had a simple conversation yesterday at the Spa". Sydni said.

"It couldn't have been too simple. This is an expensive bouquet". Said Ariel.

"Well it was just that, a simple conversation". She said.

"Then why are you getting so upset about it"? Blake asked. Sydni walked behind the bar and put her purse up.

She started washing down the bar and stocking her freezers with beer.

"She likes him". Blake and Ariel said at the same time.

That night seemed to drag by for Sydni. She messed up a few orders and had arguments with a few customers. Her nerves were on edge and all she could think about was Trevor. She called Tony, Trevor three times and they joked about it to her. She tried to ignore them but it was starting to get on her nerves. By the end of the night she couldn't wait to get home.

While they were cleaning up, the phone rang. Sydni raced to answer it thinking it might be Trevor. The call was for her but it wasn't Trevor.

"Hi Sydni, it's me Lorenzo. I came by last night to see you but you weren't there. Did you get my small offer of friendship"?

"If you are talking about this huge bouquet of flowers, yes I did get it". Sydni had a big smile on her face and she looked around and saw everyone staring at her. They all turned their heads when Sydni turned around.

"So does this mean we are friends"? Lorenzo asked.

"I guess so". She said. Sydni wrote down his phone number and promised to call him the next day. She put her bouquet in the back of her truck and went home alone.

The next few days were very hard on Sydni. Every time the phone rang she raced to it hoping that it was Trevor. It never was. She talked to Lorenzo a few times and they had worked out together that Monday. He was a good listener that helped a lot. It was Wednesday night. Sydni and Eric were just preparing to eat some pizza bread when her phone rang. She had long since given up on it being Trevor. So, she was extra surprised to hear his voice.

"Hey! What's up"? He asked.

"Nothing, how are you"? She asked.

"I'm okay I guess. I didn't want anything. So I guess I'll talk to you later". He said.

"You didn't want anything"? Said a disappointed Sydni

"No, I just wanted to say hi". He said.

"Okay well, Hi". She said as the first tear fell. Trevor could tell that she was crying.

"Okay baby, I'll talk to you later". He said and hung up.

Sydni held the phone and cried. She wanted to call him back but she didn't. She cleaned her face up and finished eating with Eric. After dinner Sydni put a movie on and she and Eric snuggled and she fell asleep.

Lorenzo was fast becoming someone Sydni talked to everyday. They had been out a couple of times but he had not met Eric. She had not met his friends or family. She brought this up one night when they had met for drinks at Fridays.

"Lorenzo, how come you've never introduced me to any of your friends? You always mention small outings that you went to with your law school friends but you never invite me".

"I don't know. It's just never come up, I guess". He said.

"What's never come up? You are always going somewhere with me and my friends. But, you never invite me to go with you anywhere. Are you afraid that they wouldn't accept me or like me"? Sydni asked.

"No, Sydni. It's not like that". He said.

"Well tell me what it's like then".

"My parents are very traditional Italians and they believe that I should marry a catholic Italian girl".

"Okay we are just friends for one, but in other words they wouldn't accept me because I'm Black. Well what about your friends"?

"My friends are just different. They aren't as open minded as I am. I just don't want you to feel out of place". Said Lorenzo.

"So you think it okay that they would judge your date because of her race"? Asked Sydni

"No I'm not saying that. It's just that, that is the way that they are. I can't try to make them change what they believe just because I don't feel the same way". He said.

"Well Lorenzo, that says something about you because there is an old adage that says "birds of a feather flock together". How can you be friends with people who discriminate against others? My friends weren't thrilled that I was dating someone of another race but they love me and accepted you as one of the gang". Sydni said.

"Well Sydni, we are just friends so why create a problem when it doesn't have to be one? It's not like I was trying to take you home to meet my mother". He said.

Sydni's mouth dropped to the floor. "What the hell does that mean"? Sydni asked.

"Sydni you know we weren't trying to hook up like that anyway". He said.

"You are right Lorenzo about one thing'. She said as she got up from the table. "I can't try to change you, so I don't even want to waste anymore of my time with a bigot. By the way, I don't think I would have wanted to meet your Mama anyway. It wouldn't have been pretty". She said as she walked away.

When Sydni got into her truck, she laid her head back on the headrest. "I guess now would be the time that I break down and cry". She thought. "I'm all cried out". She said aloud as she started the truck up and drove home.

The summer was finally over. "I made it". Sydni thought. She was registering for fall classes at Wayne State University and was feeling good about herself. She had decided to go back to school to finish her degree. She had just started a job at an Advertising Agency and knew that she could get some hands on training as an intern. Blake had registered for classes in the Business Management Program. Ariel had been offered a job in Executive Management at the bank so she was happy. Paige had registered at WSU also much to Sydni's surprise and Rimy was in her senior year.

Sydni was worried about her because she had met her newest boyfriend. He had pulled up in front of Mama's house in a souped up Monte Carlo with $2000 rims. Now where could he have gotten the money to buy those? Sydni spoke her opinion but decided to let her learn her own lessons. She remembered someone telling her that sometimes people have to stumble a few times before they walk straight. So Sydni left it alone.

She was just leaving the university when her pager went off. It was Blake. She called her back. "What's up"?

"I have a surprise for you. Guess who has tickets to the Johnny Gill concert"? Asked Blake.

"Quit playing Blake you know I love Johnny Gill". Sydni said.

'I know so I am taking you and Ariel to the concert this Saturday". Blake said.

"I'm too geeked". Sydni said.

"There's one stipulation to this. You have to be there early and you have to be dressed formally". Blake said.

What are you trying to do"? Sydni asked.

"Nothing, just be there by 7:30". Blake said.

'Alright, but not for you. I'll do it for Johnny". She said

"Girl, you are crazy. Bye". Said Blake.

For the rest of the week Sydni worried about what she would wear the night of the concert. She decided on a strapless black handkerchief dress. It hung low in the middle and the back. She paired this fabulous dress with a pair of classic Via Spiga 4-inch heels. She knew she was looking good.

Sydni pulled up to the Fox Theater and checked her watch. "I must be really early. Nobody is here yet". She rolled down her window and peeked into the theater. A doorman came to the door and opened it.

"Madame Sydni, we've been expecting you". He said.

"What"? "Madame Sydni"? Sydni said to herself. Just then another gentleman appeared at her door to park her truck. Her natural streetwise instincts almost stopped her from handing her keys over to this strange man, but she did comply.

The first gentleman opened the door and led her into an empty Fox Theater. She looked around. She had always loved the Fox, it was even more beautiful without a million people swarming all over it. She turned to the man and said.

"Are Blake and Ariel here yet"? He guided her to the VIP Dining area and told her.

"The other guests will be here momentarily". He left her sitting at a beautifully decorated table. A waiter came out and poured her a glass of champagne.

Suddenly she heard what she thought was the sound check for Johnny Gill. He was singing her favorite song "Take Me,
I'm Yours". The words to that song always made her cry. She always wished that a man would admit his faults and beg her to forgive him. A tear glistened in the corner of her eye as she thought about Trevor.

She heard footsteps and was just about to curse Blake out for being late when Trevor appeared at the top of the stairs. He looked wonderful in an Armani Tuxedo holding one red rose. Sydni covered her mouth in awe. He walked over to the table and bent down and kissed her forehead.

"Trevor", she said. "No Sydni let me talk....I've had three long months to think about what I want to say, so please let me say it". He sat down at the table.

"I cannot explain how much I miss you. I can remember everything that we've done together, every one of our conversations. I hold those memories close to my heart because I don't have any other good memories except those of my grandfather. You were there for me when nobody else was there. I need you in my life and I'm willing to do whatever I have to do to make things right. I realize now that I had a good thing and I don't want to face another day without you in my life. You make my life complete. I need you to tell me that you will give me one more chance".

Sydni looked at the man she loved. The man that she still hurt over. The tears fell down her face as she grabbed his hand.

"I can't believe you did all this". She said.

"That's what I'm telling you baby. I'm trying to change". Said Trevor

"Trevor, you don't know what pain I've felt since I watched you walk out the door that day. I've missed you too and I will always love you...but I can't come back to you. You live in a world that I cannot be a part of. There are stipulations that come with that lifestyle that I just can't deal with. I've found peace with what happened between us. And I now know that I made the right decision. You see Trevor people don't change. I know what type of person you are. My mother used to always say. "First time shame on you. Second time shame on me". I let you hurt me once before and the blame was all on you. But if I let you hurt me again. I can't blame anyone but myself".

Sydni got up from the table and pulled him up. She tasted the salt from the mixture of their tears as she kissed his lips. She hugged him hard and Lord knows she didn't want to let go, but she finally did. She couldn't look him in the face as she grabbed her purse and hurried down the stairs. She was grateful that the valet guy had left her truck in front. She looked back one last time. Trevor was standing at the top of the stairs holding that one rose.

It had been a long day. She had gone to her morning classes then had to go straight to work after that. She had picked up a pizza for Eric and herself. She was sifting through the mail when she noticed a return address from Washington D.C.. She opened the letter and recognized the handwriting immediately it was from Mya!

It read: "Hi boo! I know you are mad at me for just leaving without saying good-bye. I'm doing fine. Darius is going great. Jermaine thought it would be a good idea if we moved here because he had some relatives here that were starting a record company. (You know he Raps) he didn't want you or the girls to talk me out of it, so he planned it really quick. Don't worry about me. He has changed. He is more relaxed since we've been here. Well I have to go, he just walked in the door. Don't write. I'll write you. I love you with all of my heart. Tell everyone I said Hi. Love Mya.

Sydni couldn't stop crying. When was she gonna learn? She knew already that it was too late. Mya had never been in a healthy relationship. This was all she knew. Sydni was just grateful that he hadn't killed her yet.

That night she prayed for Mya. She prayed that the Lord would give Mya her self-esteem back, because somewhere along the way she had lost it. She asked the Lord to give her the knowledge to raise her son to become a respectful, hardworking, God-fearing man. She prayed that the Lord would give her the determination to jump the hurdles that were bound to be set before her. She prayed that the Lord would give her friends as well as herself the strength to go on.

THE END

About The Author

Erica Martin is an exciting young woman with a vision. Boundless energy and enthusiasm are some of her greatest assets. She has found a way to pursue her dream of becoming an author, while handling a busy family life with her husband and two sons, at the same time holding down a full time job. Even more amazing are her continuing efforts to complete her degree in Journalism at Wayne State University in Detroit.

At a very early stage in her life she knew that she wanted to be a writer. Her vivid imagination got her started writing poetry and short stories long before she entered High School. She was blessed to have a family that encouraged her to pursue her dreams

In preparation to write this book Erica used her own experiences as a bartender and numerous candid interviews with people that she met to understand the driving factors and other evolving issues in that world.

She is presently working in the fields of Advertising and Communication at a prestigious Design Firm as she continues her formal education.

This book addresses some of the problems that many women have personally experienced or know someone that has. The four women in this book use the power of "true friendship" loyalty and love to help each other make it through tough times. Sydni, the main character is so committed to her friendships that she often times finds herself enthralled in a web of all their problems, while still trying to balance the troubles of her own.

It is a story that will have you crying, laughing and cheering for these four ladies to attain true happiness.

Second Time ... Shame On Me.